...ough the grease-blurred
window of the bar and held his ear
close to the door to listen.

No sounds came from inside, not even the sound of breathing. Which, since those waiting for him were vampires, wasn't a surprise. He gave the door a sharp tug and the bolt tore free of the jamb, splintering wood as it came. Angel went inside, senses alert for any danger. With each step he anticipated an attack that didn't happen. Finally, in front of the bar, he found Benno's corpse, torn at the neck by sharp fangs, white from loss of blood.

The bar's front door was unlocked, so that was the escape route the vamps had taken. Maybe they hadn't meant to lay a trap at all, Angel realized. Maybe they had simply stopped to tie off a loose end after dumping the stolen truck. If that was the case then Angel was fresh out of clues, unless they'd conveniently left a map or an address inside the truck. With Wesley's life at stake, he had to check, had to try whatever he could to track them down.

Almost reluctantl_ _ _ _ _ _ _ _ _ _ _ _ _oor through which h_ _ _ _ _ _ _ _ _ _ _oor shut behind him _ _ _ _ _ _ _ _ _ _ _ _his attention. A glint o_ _ _ _ _ _ _ _ _ _ _ the projectile that flew _ _ _ _ _ _ bullet's force.

Angel™

City Of
Not Forgotten
Redemption
Close to the Ground
Shakedown
Hollywood Noir
Avatar
Soul Trade
Bruja
The Summoned
Haunted
Image
Stranger to the Sun

The Casefiles Volume 1.
The Essential Angel Posterbook

Available from Pocket Books

ANGEL™

stranger to the sun

Jeff Mariotte

An original novel based on the television series
created by Joss Whedon & David Greenwalt

POCKET
BOOKS

New York   London   Toronto   Sydney   Singapore

Historian's note: This story takes place in the second half of *Angel*'s second season.

First Pocket Books edition July 2002
™ and © 2002 Twentieth Century Fox Film Corporation.
All Rights Reserved.

POCKET BOOKS
An imprint of Simon & Schuster
Africa House
64–78 Kingsway
London WC2B 6AH

www.simonsays.co.uk

The text of this book was set in New Caledonia.

10 9 8 7 6 5 4 3 2 1

A CIP catalogue record for this book is available from
the British Library
ISBN 0-7434-4981-9

Printed in Great Britain by Cox & Wyman Ltd, Reading, Berkshire

To my father, Richard H. Mariotte,
who has taught me so much.

Acknowledgments

This one couldn't have been done without the work of some people who came before, including—but not limited to—Martin Cruz Smith, who has written so knowingly and well about coal mining, and Kevin Coyne, who knows more about what happens when the sun goes down than most of us ever will.

As always, the team at Simon & Schuster was great—Lisa, Micol, and Liz—Debbie Olshan at Fox, and all the people at Mutant Enemy who make the show go.

Thanks also to a bunch of wonderful people in the San Diego music scene who helped to inspire this story, including folks like Randi Driscol, Berkley Hart, Doug Pettibone, Eve Selis, Steve Poltz, and especially Tim Flannery, who gave me the title and let me use it.

There's a pile of coal just out back
Feeds the morning flame
Keeps us warm throughout the night
Fends off the winter's rain

We pull it from the mountainside
They pay us by the ton
God bless the black-faced miner
Strangers to the sun

—Tim Flannery
Pieces of the Past

PROLOGUE

"The Royal Shakespeare Theatre Company," Wesley said.

"The cast of *Friends*," Cordelia shot back. "Anyway, why do Sir Laurence Olivier and Sir Kenneth Branagh and all those other Sirs come to Hollywood to make their movies?"

They were sitting in the lobby of the Hyperion Hotel, Cordelia behind the counter and Wesley at one of the blue banquettes originally intended for the convenience of guests, back in the days more than twenty years ago when it had had guests. Angel was still up in his room, sleeping off a long, difficult night, though it was getting pretty late. She and Wesley had been arguing the various merits of England versus America for almost five minutes. *Which is,* Cordy thought, *about as long as we ever argue about anything without descending into juvenile name-calling.*

1

"Perhaps because movies are a low form of entertainment," Wesley tried. She could tell he was reaching. "So it only makes sense that they make more over here. You might note, however, that your American George Lucas makes his rather successful *Star Wars* films in England."

"I might," Cordelia admitted. "But then I might also note that while he's there he probably has his own chef to feed him, so he doesn't have to eat things with names like meat pies and bangers. And warm beer, what's up with that?"

"I can't really answer that one," Wesley said. "I might point out that in some parts of America, however, it's not unusual to eat raccoon and catfish and muskrat, whatever that is."

"Not the parts I frequent," Cordelia told him. "I'm sure I've never seen a muskrat, much less tasted one. Look, I'll grant you that England has some things going for it, like cool accents and Hugh Jackman—I know, he was born in Australia, but his parents were English, and aren't all the hottest English actors really Australian anyway?—but all your 'God Save the Queen' stuff will never convince me that it's a better place to live than right here in the good old U.S.A. And can I also say, since I don't see you packing a suitcase or a kit or whatever the heck you call it in English English, you must feel the same way, so stop being a big old hypocrite."

There, she'd taken the debate to the next level. Next stop, the gutter.

But they were saved from that fate by the arrival of a deliveryman at the door. He pushed it open hesitantly, which was the way most people came in, Cordy thought, since the building still looked like a hotel from the outside, but there were no signs or indications that it was one.

"Hello?" the deliveryman said tentatively. He wore the familiar forest green uniform of United Parcel Express and carried a small UPX carton. "Package for Angel Investigations."

"That's us," Cordelia said brightly, already emerging from behind the counter to sign for it. "A package. Goody. Just like Christmas."

"Yeah," the driver said without enthusiasm. She realized he delivered packages all day, every day—very few of them Christmas-like, except perhaps during the Christmas season. Which this was not.

He shoved a clipboard in front of her. "Sign here."

She signed and thanked him, and he left.

"Who is it from?" Wesley asked.

Cordelia studied the box. "Angel Investigations" was handwritten on the standard shipping label, along with the Hyperion's address. There was a return address, here in Los Angeles, but it didn't ring any bells for her. And the shipper's name was given as Bob Smith. Also no bells. "Bob Smith," she read.

"Do you know him?"

"No," Cordelia said. "Maybe Angel does."

"Perhaps," Wesley agreed.

"Let's open it."

"But if it's for Angel—" Wesley began.

Cordelia cut him off. "It's for Angel Investigations," she pointed out. "It says so right here. Just because it's his name in the title doesn't mean he's the whole agency, right?" She was, she knew, walking a thin line here. She wanted to remind Wesley that they were all part of the team without reminding him that he was the boss and could therefore order her not to open it, if he wanted to. *Not that I'd obey*, she thought. *But he could always make the attempt.*

She was about to pull the cardboard strip to open the package when the phone began to ring.

"A package and a phone call in the same day," she said, delight apparent in her voice. "This is just like a real business or something."

"Just like one," Wesley echoed.

She dropped the box in his lap as she crossed the lobby back to the counter area and the ringing phone. "You open it," she said. "But if it's anything cool, I get first dibs."

"Understood."

Cordelia caught the phone on the fourth ring. "Angel Investigations," she said. "We help the helpless."

"Greg?" the voice on the other end said.

"Excuse me, do I sound like a Greg to you?"

"Sorry." The caller hung up.

"Great," she said. "Wrong number. Watch, the package will turn out to be a wrong number too. Or a wrong name, whatever. For some other Angel Investigations we don't even know about."

"I'm sure not," Wesley replied. He yanked on the strip, breaking the seal, and pulled back the flap on the carton's side. As he did, the carton seemed to almost explode in his hands as if the contents had been under pressure inside. A cloud of greenish mist blew out in his face.

"Cor—" Wesley said. Then his eyes closed, and he slid from the banquette onto the floor, landing with a *thud*.

"Wesley!" Cordelia shouted. "Wesley, what's wrong?"

He didn't reply. She ran out from the counter area. "Angel!" she screamed, wishing he would wake up.

The vampire was already on the stairs, rubbing his eyes, dressed in a dark sweater and black pants. "I'm here," he said sleepily. "I heard the door and the phone. What happened?" Then he saw Wesley on the floor and seemed to become instantly alert.

"Don't touch him!" he warned.

Cordelia had almost reached Wesley, but something about Angel's tone stopped her in her tracks.

"What? Why? Angel, he's been gassed or some-thing."

"That's why I don't want you to touch him," Angel said. "That stuff on him . . . if that's what knocked him out, it could do the same to you."

She supposed Angel was right. And she could see Wesley breathing deep, steady breaths that made his chest rise and fall with regularity. He didn't seem to be in pain—seemed to be sleeping soundly, in fact.

"We need to get an ambulance or something, Angel. Call nine-one-one."

He joined her near Wesley. Their fallen compan-ion was surrounded by a circle of tiny green specks, almost like a bizarre dust, where the mist had set-tled. "I don't think so," he said, kneeling down. "Cover your nose and mouth with something. And don't touch this stuff."

"What is it?"

He knelt and bent over, getting as close to the edge of the mist-circle as he could without actually coming into contact with it. "From the color and texture, it looks like—"

"It looked like a cloud of mouthwash," Cordelia interrupted, feeling a sense of panic threatening to well up within her. "All minty green. Except I've never seen mouthwash make anyone faint. Do you think Wes has a fear of halitosis?"

"It's not mouthwash," Angel told her. "There's a

bit of a rainbow effect if you look at it from the right angle. It's kind of crystalline, but very fine."

"Which means what? And since when have you had a degree in chemistry?"

"Since Darla controlled me with Calynthia powder," he said. She thought she heard a trace of sorrow in his voice when he said the name of the vampire who had sired him, who he had been forced to kill, and who had later come back to life and made Angel's life hell all over again. Cordelia didn't really understand the appeal—if it had been her, she'd have been glad to get rid of the blonde bloodsucker once and for all, but Angel still seemed to have conflicted feelings about her. "I've been studying it a little," he continued. "She used it to knock me out, but with slight alterations—and in significant quantities—it can be fatal."

"You think this is one of those alterations?"

"It's very different from what she used on me. That was a pure powder. I've read that it can take various forms, including this one, but I've never personally seen it done."

"Did Darla do this?" Cordelia asked, feeling the rage burn inside her at the thought.

"Not her style," Angel said. "Look, we have to clean this stuff up, without touching it. You might breathe it in or absorb it through contact with skin. Get a vacuum cleaner or a DustBuster or something and get every speck of it up. Be very careful."

"What about Wes? Shouldn't we get him a doctor or something?"

"No human doctor is going to know what to do for him," Angel said somberly. "We need a magician or a witch or something to counter the spell. Wesley's not sick, Cordelia. He's enchanted."

Nine O'Clock

1

Angel dragged a bed into the lobby while Cordelia cleaned up the mist residue, even sucking it from Wesley's clothing with a handheld vacuum. Together, wearing rubber gloves, they unbuttoned Wesley's shirt and took it off him, since there was still some residue soaking into its threads. Then they pulled off his shoes and lifted Wesley into the bed in his pants and undershirt, tucking sheets around him and resting his head on a pillow. Cordelia removed his glasses, folded them, and set them on the banquette nearby. Through it all, Wes continued breathing deeply, like someone enjoying a pleasant sleep. Angel desperately hoped that was all it was. But he knew he couldn't count on that.

"What should I do?" Cordelia asked him. She was almost panic-stricken, pacing about the lobby, wringing her hands, her pretty face wracked with worry. "Wesley's the one who knows all the books inside and out. I can do some research online, but he's got all that specialized knowledge right at his fingertips."

"Then research," Angel suggested. "Maybe there's someone else in the city who knows about this kind of spell. Find someone who can bring him out of this."

"Angel, do you think it's really, you know . . . serious? I mean, to the point of . . ."

Angel didn't have to try hard to understand what it was she didn't want to say. "It could be fatal," he confirmed. "Or he could wake up in ten minutes. I just don't know."

"Who can we ask, then?"

"That's what you need to find out. We've met people in town, Cordy. Occultists, wizards, demons—anyone with a good grasp on magick might be able to help."

Angel left the lobby for a moment, going into his office and returning with an armload of magickal texts. Cordelia had gone to the phone.

"How about the Host?" she asked.

"Might be a good place to start," Angel agreed. As she dialed he turned to pages he'd read before, describing the effects and composition of Calynthia powder.

He scanned book after book, to no avail. There was no shortage of literature on the uses of the powder, and some information covered its manufacture. But when it came to altering it—that was where he hit a roadblock. There were any number of ways it could be altered to suit a particular magickal need, but a definite paucity of ways to counter those spells. The trick was, one needed to know precisely in what way it was altered to know how to overcome its effect.

After a little while, he realized that Cordelia wasn't on the phone anymore. He looked over and saw her sitting behind the counter, her elbows on its surface, chin resting in her hands. He hated to see her looking so gloomy.

"What happened?" he asked her.

"No luck," she reported. "The Host will ask around, try to find out anything he can. Wesley had a few other numbers in his phone book, but I'm not able to reach anyone. I've left messages with everyone I could, but you'd be surprised how many magicians don't seem to believe in simple technology like answering machines or voice mail. Maybe they get all their phone messages psychically. And by the way, Bob Smith? There are dozens in the phone book, but none at that address. That address, in fact, doesn't exist."

A different approach occurred to Angel. "Call Gunn," he said. "Get him over here."

"Gunn? Sure," Cordelia said. "There's a guy who's always hanging around the phone."

"Just call him," Angel insisted, and turned back to his books.

He *couldn't* let any harm come to Wesley. The former Watcher had turned into the nerve center of Angel Investigations—the name was the same, in fact, but Wesley was in charge now, after Angel's recent descent toward the darkness and too-slow return into the light. Whatever could be done to bring Wesley around, to protect him from the effects of the Calynthia potion—and what Angel feared most, though he kept it from Cordelia, was that the effects might be cumulative, that the longer Wesley stayed under its spell the more permanent the spell might be—had to be done. And fast.

Cordelia put down the phone again a couple of minutes later. "He's on his way," she said.

"Good." He kept his eyes on the page, looking for any helpful clues. He found nothing. Frustrated, he threw the book to the ground.

Cordelia came to his side and crouched beside his chair. She rested a hand on his arm. "I'm worried, Angel."

"So am I."

"I mean about you. I mean, I'm worried about Wes, too, of course. But you . . . you're kind of freaking me out here."

"I'm okay, Cordelia. Just concerned about him, that's all."

"Don't think I don't know you, Angel. There's more going on here than you're telling me."

He turned to face her. Her concern was evident in her dark eyes and grim expression. "Think about it, Cordelia. A box came addressed to Angel Investigations, full of some souped-up version of Calynthia powder."

"Right. And?"

"And so who do you suppose it was meant for?"

She thought about it a moment. "Could have been any of us, I guess. But probably you, you being Angel and all."

"Probably me," Angel agreed. "And not that Wesley is weak or anything, but his constitution isn't quite the same as mine."

"So what you're saying—" Realization dawned on her. "Oh! What you're saying is that if there was enough of the pixie dust in there to affect you . . ."

"It could be enough to really hurt Wes. That's right."

"Well, that's no good at all."

"That's what I've been saying," Angel said. "That's why we need to find the antidote."

Cordelia sat down next to him. "Well, quit

hogging all the books, then," she said. He put a pile of them into her hands.

They were still paging through the texts thirty minutes later when Charles Gunn showed up. "Hey, y'all," he said as he sauntered into the room. He wore an olive green sweatshirt and dark pants, and his bald head gleamed under the overhead lights. "Anne told me somethin's up."

"Something is up," Cordelia said, putting down the book she was studying, which was getting her exactly nowhere. She crossed to him and wrapped her arms around him, hugging him and drawing him across the room at the same time. He returned the embrace and then looked to where she was leading him. Angel watched his face as he noticed Wesley in the bed. Gunn's eyes widened and his jaw dropped open.

"Strange place for a nap," he suggested. "Might as well catch some Zs, that's what I always say. He could maybe use some new PJs and one of those adjustable beds from the infomercials if he's gonna start sleeping in the lobby."

"Would you still say that if he never woke up?" Cordelia asked him.

Gunn looked at Wesley again, then back at Cordelia, and finally his gaze rested on Angel. "That a real possibility?"

"A distinct one if we can't find a cure," Angel said. "He's not taking a nap; he's been poisoned. Magickally poisoned, with Calynthia powder."

"What are we sittin' around here for, then?"

"I don't think we're quite sure where to go looking," Cordelia said.

"Anyway, someone's got to stay with him," Angel pointed out. "We can't leave him alone."

"Right," Cordelia said. "And somehow I'm getting the feeling that I'm the one voted most likely to stay."

"I can," Gunn offered.

"No, I'll stay," Cordelia said. "It really does make the most sense. I mean, if you guys end up having to, I don't know, beat a confession out of somebody, or whatever, then I'm probably the least helpful."

"Don't be too sure," Gunn said, palming his own scalp. "You can whack upside the head pretty good."

"She's right," Angel said firmly, settling the matter. "She stays. Let's go."

"And anyway," Cordelia added, arms crossed and a familiar, decisive look on her face, "you couldn't get me away from Wes with a crowbar. I'll be here until he wakes up."

"That's what I figured," Angel said. He ducked into his office and found a leather duster. "Keep working the phones and do more research online. I've got my cell phone, so call if you come up with anything or if there's any change in his condition." He let that sink in a moment. "Any change at all."

Cordelia nodded, then turned back to Wesley. Angel and Gunn stepped out into the night.

2

Frank Pearsall drove the dark mountain road as fast as he could. He knew the road well, every twist and turn as familiar to him, after many years at Mount Wilson, as the inside of his own cottage on the Observatory grounds. He'd opened the window just a crack to let in some fresh mountain air, cool and pine-scented. The Angeles Crest Highway wound up through the San Gabriel Mountains above Los Angeles—hills, by Western standards, but higher than any of the so-called "mountains" east of the Mississippi—and while sometimes snow closed the road, this time of year that wasn't a problem and there was nothing but distance that could prevent the successful completion of his mission.

Frank had pizzas to deliver.

Some of the Observatory staff had taken a liking to pizza from DiGeppi's in Pasadena. But getting the pizzas up the mountain while they were still oven-fresh and hot was the kind of challenge they gave to the grad student. Frank had packed them into Styrofoam coolers, figuring that at least it would help insulate them, and as a secondary measure he'd been running the heater all the way up the mountain. Eventually, though, the blasting hot air threatened to put him to sleep, so to remain alert he'd cracked his window, letting the air wash over him

16

but, he hoped, not impacting the pizzas in their insulated box against the floorboards on the passenger side. There were always microwave ovens, but that was a last resort, to be avoided if at all possible. It rubberized the crust, Frank believed.

Finally, he hit Red Box Road and turned off the highway. From here it was only five miles to the Observatory gate. There would be little traffic, if any, from here—this time of night, the Observatory was closed to the public, who never got to see inside the domes housing the telescopes but could visit the museum, take tours, and picnic on the grounds. But of course when the sun slipped behind the horizon, the Observatory's real work was just beginning, and more staff worked night shifts than days.

Reaching the entrance, he got out of his Celica and opened the gate, then drove through and closed it behind him. Avoiding the public parking lots around the pavilion, he took the narrow road that led back to the permanent cottages and the "Monastery"—the dorm for visiting scientists and staff who didn't have cottages of their own. It was here that the pizzas were expected.

Frank got out of the car and walked around to the passenger door, opening it to retrieve the cooler. Before he did, though, he bent over it and lifted the lid just an inch, to breathe in the aroma of the six pizzas inside. They smelled heavenly, and the warm, moist air gave him hope that they had survived the trip just fine. He lifted the cooler out of the footwell, shut the door, and carried the treasure inside the dorm to the dining room. He had expected to find a crowd gathered, but there was no one in sight—in fact, he realized, he hadn't seen anyone moving about at all and didn't hear a sound now.

At first, he didn't want to call out—the building was divided in two, with half the rooms for night sleepers and half for day. But then he remembered the time. It was just a little after nine. Most of the day sleepers would not have gone to bed yet, but the night sleepers would be up, getting ready for their shifts on the equipment. So he stepped out into the silent hall. "Pizza's here!" he called. "Who's having some?"

Nobody answered.

He moved down the long central hallway, knocking on doors as he did. Still no responses, though. The building seemed empty. Frank couldn't understand that—there were times when it was largely vacant because there just weren't many visiting scientists, and those who were here were busy at one or another of the various telescopes scattered about the grounds. But he'd never been here when it was completely deserted. He couldn't raise a soul, though, so he left the pizzas inside the dining room and hiked over to the biggest of the five white domes on the mountain, housing the one hundred-inch "Hooker" telescope. This 'scope had been, for a time, the largest in the world, responsible for all sorts of important scientific advances, including Hubble's discovery of the distance scale of the universe. There should have been three people working inside tonight, observing data on the computer screens and monitors in the darkened chamber beneath the dome. Contrary to popular conception, no one actually stood with his eye to a sight on these enormous telescopes—cameras did all the looking, and the scientists and staff watched remotely. When someone did need to be in the open dome with the telescope itself, it was not glamorous duty—the night air at this elevation, particularly in winter, could be brutally cold.

At first, Frank thought this building was deserted as well. He didn't see anyone, and no one responded to his hails, although he could hear a radio playing oldies inside. But he walked in to where the people should be, and that's when he found them—Jim Dougherty, Alice Dobbins, and Albert Wu. They were all on the floor, seemingly sound asleep. He could hear their breathing from a couple of feet away, even with the music playing, could see their chests rise and fall evenly. "Hey!" he shouted. "Jim! Albert! Alice!" Nothing. He stepped closer and noticed that their clothing, faces, and the floor immediately surrounding them seemed to have been sprayed with some kind of liquid—speckle patterns remained on their skin and clothes, and on the floor. *Gassed?* he wondered. *Poisoned?* They didn't seem to be in pain, only in deep sleep. He reached out with the toe of his sneaker and jiggled Jim's foot. The scientist didn't even stir.

Frank ran from the building. He was going to have to call 911, he knew. Even though the sleepers didn't appear to him to be in any danger, he was no physician and that wasn't his area of expertise. But before he did make the call, he wanted to see just how big the problem was. He dashed from one building to the next—to the Kapetyn cottage and the other cottages, ignoring his own because he lived alone, to the long building containing the Snow solar telescope, in use since 1904 and the oldest one remaining on the mountain, the dome containing the sixty-inch telescope that dated back to 1908, the MWO twelve-incher, the hundred and fifty-foot solar tower, and the twenty-four-inch telescope. In each, he found the same thing—people sound asleep, residue of some sort of liquid spray around them. No one seemed to be hurt except maybe for Geri Inciardi, who seemed to have hit her head on a desk when she fell and got an inch-long gash.

Finally, Frank returned to the dormitory and checked some of the rooms there that he hadn't bothered to look into before. Same story here— anyone who was at home was asleep and couldn't be roused. This was some kind of attack—that was the only possible explanation, he decided. Nothing else made sense. If he'd been on the mountain instead of down collecting pizzas, he'd be a victim too. Definitely time to call in some help. With all these people out of commission, Mount Wilson, Los Angeles County's primary eye on the sky for almost a century, was effectively blind.

Stepping into the room of a staff member named Jeremy Thurston, he grabbed up the phone and dialed 911. As it rang he bent down and slapped Thurston's cheeks lightly, a last-ditch effort to wake one of the sleepers.

But when the skin of his hand touched the residue on Thurston's cheek, Frank felt like a black curtain was being drawn over his mind, and he realized his mistake. By the time the 911 operator answered, Frank had slumped over Thurston's body and was fast asleep.

3

Stanley Liebersoll had towel-dried his last plate for the night. With the dinner rush over at A Santé, the French restaurant he worked at after school, he was off duty. The restaurant stayed open until ten and there were still a couple of tables at which diners, true to the French tradition, lingered over their meals, enjoying course after course, followed by some cheese and wine, dessert and coffee. But Stanley had asked his boss, a surly, unlikable man with the distinctly not-French name of Al Houlihan, for permission to leave early tonight. To his enormous surprise and appreciation, Houlihan had agreed.

Stanley tossed his grease-stained apron into the dirty-linens bin. He'd worked at the restaurant for three years now, since his freshman year of high school. Four nights a week, including Saturday, six until eleven. It didn't do wonders for his social life, especially the part where every Saturday and most Friday nights he was busy. But then, he didn't have a girlfriend anyway, or even a terribly active dating calendar. While he recognized that working here limited his chances of meeting anyone dateworthy— or, more accurately, anyone who would consider him dateworthy since, like most males, he was sure, his primary criteria for judging the appeal of any given female was how attracted to him she might be—he also knew that his family needed the money he brought in, and that whole finishing-high-school thing was pretty much dependent on him helping out with the monthly bills.

His dad worked as a security guard at a shopping mall, volunteering for the night shift because of the ten percent pay differential, and his mom did telephone sales work and watched Stanley's two little sisters, but even with two incomes they lived from day to day, never quite sure if they were going to be able to both make the rent on their apartment and eat three meals a day. Stanley got to take home leftovers from the restaurant sometimes, and his paychecks helped make ends meet, so the job wasn't something he could just walk away from even though Houlihan was the world's biggest grump sometimes.

The family's combined income rarely allowed for anything like going to a movie or sporting event, though they owned an old VCR and sometimes managed to rent semirecent flicks. Tonight, though, Stanley had plans. He had been given a free pass to a rave. Folded over and safely tucked in the rear pocket of his black jeans was the pass, which he'd taken out and looked at a dozen times tonight. The design was a crazy mixture of super-contemporary typeface, so trendy it was barely legible, with sixties-style op art and fifties black-and-white TV-show modern. In the center of the card, a traditional nuclear family sat on a couch, dad and son in crew-cuts and mom in pearls, all decked out in their 3-D glasses. Black-and-white lines strobed out from that image, interspersed with single words in floating balloons. "Fun!" one promised. "Keen!" "Nifty!"

At the bottom was the name DJ Killz, an address, and the words "Admit One." One of the waiters, Colin Embry, a guy three or four years older than Stanley who studied film at USC, had given him the pass, saying that he'd received it from one of the rave's organizers but he wasn't going to be able to make it. A Santé was in Burbank and the rave was in Downey, so Stanley would be spending a good part of his evening on a bus. But there was no way he was going to pass up a night of dancing and who-knew-what-else, all for free. So he'd gotten permission from his parents, and Al had agreed to let him leave early, and he was on his way.

This would, he was certain, be a night to remember.

4

Wesley was handed a glowing lantern with the number 127 scratched on its base, its small flame enclosed within a cylinder of wire gauze. He had barely grasped the handle when other men jostled past him to get their own. All were dressed in black, as he was, he noticed, with strange clog-like shoes, metal-rimmed at the bottom almost like horseshoes. His jacket felt like wool, scratchy and stiff, and his pants were moleskin, patched at the knees. Like the others, he wore a cloth cap on his head, and a tin hung from a strap that crossed his chest. He jostled it, wondering what was inside. *Food, maybe, but not water,* he thought. In one of his pockets he could feel a flask of some liquid that he suspected was water, though he hadn't opened it to check.

"No," he said suddenly, feeling a sense of panic well up in him. "No. This is not right. I don't belong here."

"Where d'ya belong then?" someone asked him. "In London with the queen?"

Others laughed at that and continued on, reaching out for their lanterns.

"I belong . . . I . . . ," Wesley began. But he realized he didn't know the answer himself. Anyway, the tide of men was moving him farther and farther from the fellow who'd handed him the lantern. No one else seemed to be in charge of anything—they were, like him, just taking their lanterns and moving on. With no apparent options, unable to fight the current of humanity, Wesley allowed himself to drift with the flow of the throng, out of the lantern room and into a vast dark chasm.

He was, he realized, in a mine—most likely a coal mine, now that he thought about it and looked around at the clothing, the dark walls, the fine layer of soot on everything. He didn't know why he should be in a coal mine, dressed just like the other miners . . . but he couldn't think of any reason why he shouldn't, either. Some unformed thought nagged at him, but it was stuck in a remote corner of his brain and he couldn't dislodge it.

The flood of men led him across the cavern to a

steel elevator cage. There seemed no way around it, so he crowded into the cage with the others. Some of the men joked and laughed with each other, and they pressed against each other, filling every square inch of the cage, with the easy familiarity of men who face danger together on a regular basis. Their accents were rough, almost archaic-sounding. *Lancashiremen,* Wesley thought at first. But he quickly realized that he wouldn't have been able to understand the thick, strange accents of working-class Lancashiremen. This was something else—Yorkshiremen, he guessed, but from some time in the past. Again, he had a vague sense that there was something wrong with that explanation, but he couldn't pinpoint what it might be.

When the cage was beyond full, someone on the outside—Wesley couldn't even see who, so dim was the lighting in this place—hooked a couple of chains across the open end. *No stepping off now,* he thought.

With a jolt, the descent began. It felt like free fall. The lift rumbled, air rushed past, but they fell into solid blackness, so there were no visual cues he could use to judge their speed. The miners around him didn't pause in their conversations, so it seemed to be second nature to them, but Wesley found himself hoping there was some adequate braking mechanism to slow them when they reached bottom—however far down that might be. Some of the old coal mines, he knew, could be as much as a mile deep. *By the end of a mile-drop this cage could be moving pretty fast.*

As they dropped, Wesley looked at the miners around him, lit by the glow of their combined lanterns. Once they reached the bottom and spread out, he feared, the faint light coming from each would be insufficient to illuminate much more than the hand that held it, or a single face if it was lifted close. But together on the rocking, plummeting car, they combined to cast a light that revealed gaunt, weary men, faces scrubbed for the day but nonetheless blackened by years in the pits. Where they were scarred, coal dust had worked its way under their skin, tattooing them. Their eyes were reddened from the constant exposure. *England runs on coal,* Wesley thought. *The world runs on coal.* But the price paid by these men—and their likes in Lancashire and Cork, Alsace and the Ruhr, Pennsylvania and Kentucky, and wherever else ancient vegetation slowly hardened into the precious black rock—was high indeed. Black lung awaited many, perhaps most, if they survived the dangers of working deep underground surrounded by the highly flammable mineral.

He didn't belong here, he knew. But somehow, although it didn't feel right for Wesley to be going down into the pit, it didn't feel wrong either. At any rate, there didn't seem to be much of a choice. The elevator began to slow, and then it came to a stop and the men spilled out. Wesley followed suit. Momentarily someone shoved a wood-handled pick into his hands, and he found himself trailing along down a tall shaft, the ceiling of which was lost in the blackness around him, along with the other miners.

He understood now, as clearly as if he'd been told, what the number on his lantern was for. Each miner would have a different number, so that at the end of the day, the mine's managers would know that as many men who went in also found their way out. Thousands of tons of rock hung over him here, he knew, with maybe as much as a mile of the Earth's crust suspended above him. He didn't know how deep this one was, but guessed it was deep. It was stupefyingly hot, for one thing, like walking through God's own blast furnace.

Like walking through Hell.

Ten O'Clock

1

"I don't mean to sound disrespectful, Angel," Gunn said. "But do you got any idea where we're goin'?"

"Magick shop," Angel replied. He turned the GTX's wheel, screaming around a corner, and bore down on the accelerator even before completely coming out of the turn. The car lunged forward, hurtling up Robertson. Other cars pulled out of the way.

"For what?"

"Supplies. More books."

"But do you know what you're doing? Don't you need to know what kind of spell you're tryin' to pull off before you go shopping for the ingredients?"

"There are a finite number of ways to counteract Calynthia powder," Angel told him. He realized he was gripping the steering wheel so tightly that his knuckles were white. But then again, keeping out of the sun for a couple of hundred years pretty much made you pale all over. Still, he loosened his grip just a little. "We'll lay in whatever we might need, so when we figure out precisely what to do we'll be ready to do it. In the meantime, Rick's might have some more books. Maybe Rick himself will have some guesses."

"This the same Rick who Cordelia claims sold her the wrong kind of magick box?"

Angel nodded, remembering his failed attempt to contain an Ethros demon in a Shorshack box. "He's a huckster. You can't always trust him when he wants to make a sale. But he knows his stuff, generally. And he's well-stocked on the things we'll need."

"Yeah, well, I'm all out of newt eyes myself," Gunn said. "So I guess I'm up for it. Long as we're on Melrose, though—no, never mind, probably not a good night for it."

"Probably isn't," Angel agreed. "But you brought it up. What's on your mind?"

Gunn cleared his throat and looked out the car's window for a moment.

"Gunn," Angel said, putting a hint of menace in his voice.

"Well, I was readin' these comic books Rondell had. You know, superheroes and all that. Fightin' crime, rightin' wrongs."

"Self-improvement regime?" Angel asked.

"I didn't say it was high culture," Gunn said. "He just had 'em, and I was flippin' through 'em, you know? Nostalgia."

"I'm nostalgic for different things," Angel said. "Sunlight. Food. The green, rolling hills outside Galway."

"I can dig it," Gunn said. "But these comics, they were nostalgic for me. Stuff I used to read in my own misspent youth. And it got me thinkin'."

Angel glanced at him as he rounded a corner. "Why does that sound like a bad combination?"

"You do all that stuff," Gunn said. "Fight crime, right wrongs, the whole bit. You think maybe it'd be easier if you traded in the black duster, got some kind of costume, maybe a scary-ass name like Dark Avenger or The Stomper or something? Because, as names go, I'm sorry, man, but Angel ain't all that scary."

"Why does everyone keep telling me that?" Angel replied tersely. "No. No costume, no new name."

"But see, the idea is to strike fear into the hearts of evildoers. They fear the costume and the name, your job is that much easier when you finally get to 'em."

"The ones I'm concerned about are mostly afraid of me already," Angel explained. "The ones who aren't learn to be."

"Yeah, I guess that's a point," Gunn relented. "Those superheroes in the comics, they have a lot more repeat business than you do. Supervillains never really die."

"I try to kill them so they stay dead," Angel said. He slid the car around a sharp turn, fishtailing a little. From the corner of his eye he noticed Gunn gripping the door handle. He hoped that was the end of the conversation.

Costumes, he thought. *Me in Spandex? I don't think so.*

A few moments later, Angel pulled off Robertson and parked in an alley a half block from Melrose. When Angel was in a hurry he liked to jump out of the car, but it had last been driven in daylight and he hadn't wanted to waste the time tonight to take the roof down.

Even at this hour Melrose was its typical self— packed with a wide cross-section of humanity, from goggle-eyed tourists to punks sporting foot-tall green spiked Mohawks to the pierced and tattooed who made their bodies into living canvases for their unique art. Rick's Majick 'n' Stuff served the casually curious and the serious magickal community equally, and the front window welcomed the former with an unthreatening display of candles and crystals. The serious stuff, Angel knew, was in the back, behind the counter. He pushed open the door, and a bell tied to its handle jingled softly in the quiet store.

There was no one in sight inside. "Rick?" Angel called.

"Looks like he made himself disappear," Gunn observed. "Typical magician, I guess."

"He wouldn't leave the shop unattended," Angel said, walking deeper into the interior of the large shop. The store was neatly laid out, everything clean and dusted, everything in its place. It didn't look like a place that had been abandoned for long.

"Lots of people on the street, but no browsers in here," Gunn said. "It's a quiet night, maybe he ran down to the corner for a cup of coffee or something."

"Rick isn't big on the honor system," Angel said. "Let's look around."

They didn't have to look for long.

"Check it out," Gunn said, pointing to the floor behind the sales counter. Angel joined him, leaning over the counter. Rick was crumpled in a heap on the floor. His breathing was steady, but he was apparently lost in a deep sleep.

"Just like Wesley," Angel said.

And just like Wesley, there was an opened UPX carton beside him, and a dusting of fine green specks everywhere.

2

Jacquelyn Kirby's date had gone pretty well. Blair Caswell was older than she—*a lot older,* she thought, over thirty, while she was just nineteen. That didn't bother her a whole lot. She was used to dating older men, used to being chased by them, in fact, and had no problem with helping them spend their money. And Blair Caswell apparently had plenty of it. During dinner Wolfgang himself had come out of the kitchen to see them—mostly Blair, it seemed, but she got to bask in a little of the reflected glory.

He wasn't as wealthy as her dad, by any means. Blair was Brentwood, but her dad was Bel Air. Yet while Jackie had an allowance, of course, and a generous one, Dad's money wasn't necessarily the same thing as *her* money. So there was something to be said for letting men spend theirs when a girl wanted a nice meal or a good time. Blair was an entertainment lawyer-slash-producer, on the fast track. He was tennis-club handsome, kind of funny, interesting enough for an old guy. He drove a Beemer, which wasn't the same thing as driving a Porsche but way better than those who drove Hummers, who were, as far as Jackie was concerned, simply compensating for some other shortcoming. If his name hadn't been Blair he would have been a pretty worthwhile date. There had been two girls in her high school named Blair, one Blaire with an "e" on the end, neither one somebody of whom she particularly wanted to be reminded. And what was up with a guy having a girl's name? That in itself guaranteed that marriage wasn't happening here, not that she was looking for someone to marry in the first place. She couldn't imagine a lifetime with a man named Blair. She had a hard time imagining a second date, but there was still time for that to change.

Because, in spite of the fact that dinner had been leisurely and Spago lovely and full of minor celebrities, Jackie was a late-night kind of girl and a long way from being ready to call it a night. She knew where there was a rave over in Downey, and while Blair seemed about the least likely guy to have a good time at a rave, if he wanted to be with her when the sun came up he was going to have to try.

"Turn here," she said. She was directing him to her house. One dressed differently for a rave than for dinner at Spago, and she was a firm believer in always dressing for the occasion. She had her own entrance at home, around at the side of the house, so she wouldn't even have to see her parents again tonight. They knew she wasn't expecting to be home until morning, and if they had any problem with it they were wise enough to keep it to themselves.

"Listen, are you sure this is what you want to do?" Blair asked. "I know an all-night club in Venice where we could have drinks, listen to some nice music, maybe a cigar—"

"I'm not twenty-one," she reminded him. "So drinks are out, unless you're advocating breaking the law, which I'm sure you, an officer of the court, are not. And I want to dance, not listen to some

Kenny G impersonator play light jazz. I'm in the mood to party. If you don't want to play, you can just drop me off outside when we get there—the rave, not my folks' house. I'm sure I can catch a ride home."

"No," Blair said quickly. "I was just offering a suggestion. I'll go in with you. Sounds kind of fun, actually."

Yeah, she thought, *like major dental work is fun. You have no idea what you're in for, Blair old chum. No idea at all.*

3

Angel opened the cash register drawer. There was plenty of cash in it, so Rick didn't seem to have been robbed. Yet. But he wouldn't give odds that the situation would remain that way for long, with Rick out of action and nobody else minding the store.

He stepped past Rick and went through the double doors that led into the shop's storage area. The arrangement was simple—books in one area, spell ingredients in another, implements in labeled drawers, crystals in tall transparent cabinets. Even though he'd been hoping that Rick might have some suggestions, Angel already had a good idea of what he needed, so he grabbed a couple of shopping bags and began loading them up.

A few minutes later he emerged. Gunn stood with his hands in his pockets, looking out the front window toward the street beyond.

"Let's find a cop," Angel said. "Melrose is usually crawling with them."

"Why do we need a cop?" Gunn asked him. "If this is the same thing that happened to Wes, a cop's not gonna help him."

"Someone has to stay in the store, to make sure it's not robbed," Angel said.

Gunn indicated the books and supplies Angel had bagged from the back room. "Like you just did, you mean."

"I'll settle up with him later for these. If I can break the spell, it'll help him, too."

"We can't just lock the door behind us?"

"I didn't see keys anywhere and I don't want to hunt for them. They might be in his pocket, but we can't touch his body without cleaning him off first. We don't have time for that. If we can't find a cop in a hurry then we'll call it in from the road."

They exited the store, Angel looking up and down Melrose while Gunn ran the merchandise to the GTX. As Angel had hoped, a black-and-white cruiser was just up the street with a single officer inside, who pulled over when Angel flagged him down. Angel explained the situation to the officer, whose name badge said Ruiz, as briefly and vaguely as he could, and the cop radioed in for an ambulance.

Then he left his car at the curb and followed Angel inside.

"He's behind the counter," Angel said. "Don't go near him or touch the residue."

"I tell you how to do your job?" Ruiz asked. He was a tall Hispanic man with a tiny mustache like an old-fashioned banker's. He went around the counter.

"I'm just telling you, you don't know what you're dealing with."

"Sounds like maybe you know a little too much about it," Ruiz speculated. "But to me, it looks like I'm dealing with a guy who sniffed a little too much of his own shipment." He bent over Rick, disappearing from Angel's sight. "Weird looking stuff, though. Maybe some new hybrid. Narcotics is going to want to see this. . . ."

"Don't!" Angel warned again. But the cop let out a soft moan, and then Angel heard the rustle of his body collapsing over Rick's. He hurried to the counter, but too late. So that Ruiz wouldn't crush Rick, Angel dragged him by the feet, where the mist hadn't settled, until the cop's sleeping body was clear of the shop owner.

The bell on the door rang and Angel rose. It was just Gunn, returning from the car.

"What happened to your policeman friend?"

"He wanted to sample the Calynthia," Angel told him. "I tried to warn him."

"You know, Angel, this is just gonna keep happening. You want to spend your whole night here watching the bodies pile up?"

"You're right," Angel said. "Anyway, there's an ambulance on the way. They'll figure it out eventually. Let's just get out of here."

On the way out the door, he turned the sign around so it read CLOSED and hoped that between that and the squad car parked outside, people would leave the store alone. But realistically he expected that the problem would get worse before it got better—other police officers would come along, see the car, and come inside to investigate. He could only hope that the paramedics who came would understand that the residue worked through contact and would use care tending to the victims.

The more discouraging thing, though, was the fact that Rick had received a package just like the one that Angel Investigations had. He had even checked the return address, and this one was also sent by the mythical "Bob Smith." That meant it wasn't an isolated incident—in fact, since there had been two such deliveries that Angel was aware of in the space of an hour, chances were there were more that he didn't know about yet.

This had gone, suddenly, from a concern about Wesley to a wider problem—the scope of which Angel had no idea. But it was beginning to look like a busy night lay ahead.

4

Cordelia felt a twinge of pain behind her eyelids and almost wept with joy. *Come on, vision,* she thought. *Good time for a vision. Great time, even.* Because with a vision would come a clue, and clues were what they were short of so far. Visions were just the thing they needed to point them in some direction or other, to get them on the right track. Any track at all would do right now, because so far she not only hadn't had a track to work on, she wasn't even sure there was a train. *There's nothing like a good old vision,* she thought, *to really make a girl's night.*

The first thing she had done after Angel and Gunn had left her alone with Wesley had been to kiss him. They'd kissed before. When he'd first arrived in Sunnydale to be Faith's Watcher, during her senior year, she'd thought there was something charming and maybe a little dashing about him, what with the whole British accent and Watcher training thing. They had danced together at her prom and kissed afterward in the library, but the kiss proved less than satisfactory— proved, in fact, that despite mutual attraction there was no real chemistry going on at all.

Nonetheless, when he had arrived in Los Angeles, no longer a Watcher but now a "rogue demon hunter," as he put it, clad in leather, she greeted him with another passionate kiss. This one, though, was a failed attempt to transfer to him the vision power Doyle had left her—also with a kiss. It didn't take, though. The visions were just hers to deal with, and there seemed to be nothing she could do about it. That kiss had surprised him, but at least he had kissed back.

Tonight, though—nothing. Not even a lip wiggle. Cordelia was used to being sought after, desired. She couldn't remember a time when she'd kissed someone and had absolutely zero response. Of course, Wesley was unconscious, which certainly had a lot to do with it. But still she felt a twinge of disappointment. She was no Princess Charming, but she'd given it a shot, just in case her kiss was sufficient to wake Wes.

When that didn't work, she parked herself at her desk, surfing the Internet. References to Calynthia powder were surprisingly common, but most of them were just glancing mentions, with no real meat to them. A couple led her to more detailed descriptions, but, like the books they'd already consulted, there was no solid information on how to undo the powder's effects if it had been manipulated in an unknown way.

Shouldn't there be some kind of "Ask Merlin" site where you can find answers to common household magick questions? she thought. *I mean, who needs the 'net if it's all pictures of Britney Spears and downloadable *NSYNC songs? It's not like you can get away from those in the real world.*

Suddenly she heard a groan from the bed, and she turned away from the computer in time to see Wesley shift position, turning from his back onto his side. This was the first time he'd moved since she and Angel had tucked him in. She hurried to his side.

"Wesley?" she said hopefully.

His face was pinched, his brow furrowed as if anxiety was rearranging his handsome features. She touched his shoulder and wiped a sheen of sweat from his forehead. "Wesley, is there anything I can do? A triple espresso, maybe? English breakfast tea?"

He didn't answer, just let out another quiet moan and shivered once. His eyes twitched rapidly.

He's dreaming, she thought. *Not waking up, just dreaming.*

She hoped it was a good dream. He might as well be enjoying his rest. She rubbed her temples, aware now that there was no vision on the way after all, but just a tension headache from worry and from staring at the computer screen. Headache or not, there was nothing else to do but get back to it.

5

Carrying his pick and his lantern, Wesley followed the other miners deep into the tunnel. The shaft with the elevator was far behind him somewhere, lost in the darkness. Down here there was only coal and the men working to take it from the earth, and the ponies hauling tubs of it back to the elevator. A stiff, hot wind blew past him, part of a ventilation system designed to keep the air breathable and the explosive gases dissipated. Details came to him now, snippets of information he had known and filed someplace in his brain, returning to prominence now as if they were everyday facts. The lamp he held, and the ones hanging from wooden timbers every few meters down the tunnel, were brass, with brass gauze in the middle to keep the flame cool enough not to ignite the gases. Cutting the coal released methane, he thought he remembered. Miners used explosives, sometimes, to loosen walls of coal, or veins of it, especially when it was old and deep and hard to break. But care had to be paid because if the methane buildup was too high and someone touched off an explosive or opened a lantern to see better or even struck a match to light a cigarette, then the entire shaft could become a sudden inferno. Fire was no joke down in the shaft.

He flattened himself against a wall to let a pony go by, dragging full tubs of coal, tied together in a sort of train, behind it. A boy led the pony. *He can't be older than ten,* Wesley thought. *Ten, and already down in the pits.* Except for the occasional day off, and Christmas, the boy might never see the sun. Miners walked to work in the dark, before the sun rose, and by the time their shift was over the sun had set again. Even during the day, in a coal town, smoke and soot hung over the sky like a shroud, blackening every surface. Wesley tried to remember the sun, tried to picture a clean ocean with sunlight sparkling off the water, but couldn't quite bring it into focus.

"You movin' on or spendin' the day here?" a miner asked him.

"Sorry," Wesley said. He hadn't realized that he was still standing next to the wall. In the dark, with only his faint lantern glowing, the man had almost walked right up into him. "I'm not really sure where I'm supposed to be."

"I look like a foreman t'you?" the man replied.

Wesley studied him, though he understood the question was rhetorical. He was confused—part of him felt like he'd been in the pits his whole life, just like the boy with the pony would certainly be. But so much of it seemed new and unfamiliar. It was a disorienting feeling.

"No," he said finally. "You don't."

"You don't have anything better to do, there's a vein off in t'other shaft, just ahead," the man said. "I've been workin' it wi' Paddy, but he cut his leg yesterday and's stayin' home."

For just a second, something about the man seemed familiar to Wesley. He couldn't place what it was, though—the man looked like all the other black-faced, red-eyed miners. *We were probably just in the lift together,* he thought. *I'm sure that's it.*

"Certainly," he said, glad to at least have a place to work and perhaps someone to talk to. "I'll go with you."

"Come on, then," the man said. "They're not payin' us just for spendin' time down here. There's coal to find."

He moved off in the dark, walking quickly, back bent to keep him hunched over and his head clear of the unseen timbers above. Wesley followed the man's swinging lantern as quickly as he could, the clogs on his feet slowing his progress and making him walk with an awkward, rolling gait. The man led him deep, deeper into the mine's black belly, like eternal starless night.

Eleven O'Clock

1

Angel spun the GTX's wheel and pulled the car over to the curb, braking hard enough to make both of them lurch forward against their seat belts. He halted the car in the valley of darkness between the glowing pools of light created by two tall street lamps. Traffic was minimal, with most daytime residents of the city already home and in bed, and those out for the night still ensconced in bars or nightclubs, so the sudden stop wasn't as dangerous as it would have been earlier in the day.

Gunn stared at Angel. "What's up?" he asked.

"We need to separate," Angel said flatly. Anxious to be in motion, he hadn't taken his hands from the wheel. "We can cover more ground apart than together."

"That's true," Gunn said. "But what ground do we need to cover? You got your stuff from the magick shop, Cordy's doin' research. . . . Where do you want me to go?"

"You go check out the address from the package," Angel instructed. "Bob Smith's address."

"I thought Cordy said it didn't exist," Gunn reminded him.

"That's right. But maybe there's someone in that area who knows something. We can't afford to skip a single clue, no matter how tenuous. It's not just Wesley's life at stake anymore. We don't know how many packages this nonexistent Bob Smith sent out."

Gunn shrugged and climbed out of the convertible. "I'll try to track down old Bob, then," he agreed.

Angel reached into his duster's inner pocket and withdrew a piece of paper that Cordelia had printed out. He unfolded it and tore off a section. "Here," he said, handing the section to Gunn. "When you're finished looking for Bob, visit these people. These are some of the names from Wesley's contact list. People in the L.A. area who have some connection to the occult. We need to find out what they know, if they can help us with an antidote, and if they've been attacked too then we need to know that. I'll take the rest of the list. Call me if you learn anything and check in with Cordy at the hotel once in a while so we can keep tabs on each other."

Gunn pocketed his portion of the list. "I'm on it, but it'd be easier if you dropped me at my truck," he said as he left the GTX, "or if I had a special car. Some kind of Gunn-mobile, maybe—"

"Don't start with the costumes again," Angel warned him.

"—but I'll cope."

Angel was already pressing his foot down on the accelerator. "Take a cab," he called behind him. *Gunn's nothing if not resourceful*, he thought. *He'll figure something out.*

2

Finding that Rick at the magick shop had been attacked changed Angel's priorities. Before he had wanted nothing more than to get back to the hotel with the books and the ingredients he had picked up and set about trying to find an antidote. But the fact that more people than just Wesley had been attacked meant his approach had to be altered, and he needed to be flexible enough to go with it. Not knowing in what way the Calynthia powder had been altered meant that there would be a lot of trial and error involved in coming up with an antidote. If he could save others from falling under the powder's spell, it was possible that one of them could help with the work. Even Rick was more proficient at magick than Angel was—Angel's first response was usually more related to hitting and kicking than spell casting. So instead of going straight home, he decided to work part of the list.

The first name on Angel's section of the list was Dr. Ravi Tirunagaru. Angel had never met Tirunagaru but had heard Wesley speak of him from time to time. He was a well-known Indian physicist, mystic, and philosopher who wrote weighty metaphysical treatises from a two-bedroom apartment in West Hollywood. Angel took Sunset most of the way down, passing row after row of closed shops with apartments above them. Inside some of those, people tried to keep the night at bay with miniature suns, lamps casting yellow-and-white light through windows, or the bluish glow of televisions. Here and there a late-night coffee shop or club was open, and clumps of young people stood together under street lights looking for something to do, somewhere to go. On one corner a power-company crew worked under the glare of bright floodlights. But for the most part the city was giving way to the night.

Finally Angel neared Tirunagaru's address and parked on the street a block away, in front of a twenty-four-hour market. Walking toward the doctor's building, he noticed a truck idling by the curb, and then saw a uniformed UPX deliveryman emerge from the front door of Tirunagaru's building, headed for the truck.

Something's not right, Angel realized immediately. *UPX doesn't make deliveries this late at night.* Sure, the company had trucks rolling back and forth between distribution centers and the airport, but not individual pick-ups or drop-offs at private residences. Added to the fact that the packages that had felled Wesley and Rick had both been UPX packages, a connection seemed certain. He started to run.

3

Homer heard rapid footfalls coming toward him. *Mugger,* he thought instantly, looking toward the source of the sound. He'd already made his delivery, his hands were empty, but what did that matter to some crackhead or junkie out for a quick buck to feed his habit? Not that a small-time crook worried him—in fact, if he weren't on such a tight schedule he'd appreciate the distraction.

But the man coming at him didn't look like a mugger. He was tall and powerful, with dark hair and a long black coat. The expression on his face was one of quiet determination and distinct menace.

Homer dashed for the truck, which stood idling at the curb. "Go!" he shouted to Lenny, behind the wheel. "Go! Go!"

Lenny shifted into gear and the truck was already rolling when Homer hurled himself through the air, off the sidewalk, and in through the open passenger door. He fell against the metal floor and bashed himself into the seat. "Fast!" Homer said, winded. "He's almost on us!"

"Who is?" Lenny asked. "What are we running from?"

"I think . . ." Homer hesitated, almost unwilling to say it. "I think it's Angel."

"Angel? The vampire Angel? That ain't possible."

In that instant, Homer hated his partner. Lenny was always so sure of everything, so convinced that he knew what was what, what was going on. "It's *possible* that you're a moron," Homer said with a low snarl. "Drive the truck. Get out of here."

Lenny drove—that was one thing he did do well. He up-shifted, running quickly and efficiently through the gears. As Homer hoisted himself into his seat, he saw that traffic was light, a few cars on the road but not many, not enough really to get in their way. He risked a glance at Lenny, dressed as usual in his traditional baggy shorts and oversized sweatshirt. He didn't even look like a UPX driver. At least Homer had put on the uniform, trying to make things look normal. The most he'd been able to persuade Lenny to do was put on a hat. "You're the one leaving the truck," Lenny had said. "Ain't no one gonna see me."

Homer had given up then. He'd never actually won an argument with Lenny. They just rolled on and on to ridiculous lengths, and then turned into some other argument altogether. He always stopped trying after a little while, savoring small victories where he found them, as with the hat.

As they put block after block behind them, Homer started to relax a little. He was about to lean out the open door, to look back and see if he could spot Angel in the distance, when he heard a thump at the back of the truck.

"He's here," he said. "I thought I told you to drive."

4

When Angel broke into a run, the deliveryman was almost at the truck. He saw Angel coming toward him and shouted something to its driver. The truck was already in motion when the uniformed man jumped through the open door. The truck picked up speed fast, with little traffic on the wide, empty street to impede its progress.

Angel knew he couldn't let the truck get away. He

had no doubt now that the truck was the key to whatever was going on. The way they were running proved that. Which also meant there was little if any doubt that Dr. Tirunagaru was also the recipient of a toxic package, and that his package had just been delivered.

First things first, Angel thought. He could check in on the physicist later. But now, he needed to catch that truck.

His feet flew. He was taking a gamble—if it turned out he needed his car to catch the UPX truck, then he was running the wrong way and would just give them more time to make their escape. But he believed he could catch the truck before they got too far or gained too much speed, while going back for the car might give them a big enough lead that he'd never find them. So he ran, and ran fast.

Ahead, a traffic light changed to yellow and red, and the few cars out on the road came to a stop. The UPX truck, Angel noted, didn't stop with the rest. It slowed and swerved to the right, bouncing up over the curb and continuing into the intersection, two wheels on the sidewalk, dodging the cars stopped in front of it. A few cars sped through the intersection on the cross street, so the UPX truck had to slow for a moment, letting them pass. As soon as the way was clear, though, the truck was in motion again, without waiting for the light to turn green.

The pause gave Angel the time he needed to catch up. He kept up his flat-out pace the whole time and hit the intersection just as the light flashed green. The UPX truck was still working on gaining speed again after the stop, closing in on the next intersection. The light there was green. Once the truck was through that intersection, they'd have enough speed to lose him. Angel could hear the driver shifting up as the man tried to coax every bit of power from the engine. He was close enough now to taste the exhaust, to see the stains of city wear on the truck's green-and-white paint job. As the truck began to pull away from him again, Angel leaped.

One foot landed on the truck's rear bumper and his left hand closed on the handle of the back door. The rocking motion of the truck threatened to throw him, but he held on, firming his grip as he developed the next part of his plan. He would just stay with the truck until it stopped again, and then he would take down the driver and the other delivery-man and get some answers. He was a long way from comfortable but he thought he could hang on for a while, protected by the truck's bulk from the worst of the wind. Passing motorists stared at him as if he were insane, and there was certainly, he knew, some merit to that idea. But he didn't plan to lose these guys now that he had found them.

Then the truck's rear door swung open, nearly

dislodging him from his precarious perch. He grabbed onto the top of the door and held on, swinging out with it. The hinges creaked and Angel glanced down to see the street rushing past his feet. Inside the truck, the uniformed delivery guy crouched, holding something that was undeniably a weapon, although one Angel had never seen before. More than anything else, it resembled a flare gun, with a wide, round barrel, pointed right at him. The guy had a finger over the trigger.

The guy's face, Angel realized, had changed in the past few minutes—his forehead bulging and furrowing, his jaw elongating, his teeth becoming menacing fangs.

The guy's a vampire.

The delivery vamp squeezed the trigger, barrel still pointed toward Angel, and some kind of projectile flew from it. Angel let go of the swinging door, falling from the truck and hitting the pavement hard. He rolled to a stop against the curb. When he was able to look up again, mentally cataloging the bruises and scrapes he'd earned, he saw that the truck had continued down the street. The projectile had sailed harmlessly past him and shattered on the street, well behind him. Where it had hit, a cloud of greenish gas hung in the air, like steam over a manhole cover in winter.

Half a block away, the truck's brake lights came on. It stopped, then started again more slowly, pulling into an intersection and making a U-turn. Having reversed its direction, it roared straight at Angel.

He made it to his feet before it reached him, and dove out of its way, up onto the sidewalk, colliding with a metal newspaper box and a concrete waste-can fixture. He ducked behind the big cement box, where the truck couldn't get him.

The truck came to a stop, and the driver leaned out his window. Like the delivery guy, the driver was in full vamp mode. Angel let the change come across his own features, just in case these guys didn't know what they were dealing with.

The driver watched him change and smiled. The other guy put the flare-gun-type weapon into the driver's hand. He pointed it at Angel and pulled the trigger. Angel jumped straight up, a vertical leap that took him to the landing of a fire escape a dozen feet overhead, as the "flare"—really, he guessed, a concentrated dose of the same green Calynthia mist—hit the ground where he'd just been and exploded. Anyone within ten feet of the spot would have been overcome instantly, he knew. As it was, he worried that he might have gotten some on the soles of his boots.

As the driver reloaded, Angel leaped again, jumping from the fire escape to the roof of the truck, and then bounding down to the other side. But the second vamp waited there with a flare gun of his own.

Angel dodged again, but the shot came closer this time as the guy anticipated his move. Angel glanced at the windows nearby—all the lights had gone out, as if any observers who weren't asleep wanted to pretend that they were. There was no help coming from anywhere.

I can't get close to the truck as long as they have all that Calynthia powder, Angel thought. Allowing himself to be knocked out would be the worst possible thing he could do—he'd be useless to Wesley then, and everyone else as well. So even though it would ordinarily have been his last resort, he turned his back on the truck, jumping back up to the fire escape and climbing the ladder to the building's roof, blending into the shadows there above the glow of streetlamps. The truck idled on the street for a few minutes, both the driver and his partner scouring the street and the shadows for any sign of Angel. Eventually, the vampires gave up and drove away. Angel watched it go regretfully. *Spider-Man could have followed it,* he thought, *swinging from building to building on his web. But not me.* For now, Angel was defeated.

Maybe there's some merit to Gunn's superhero idea after all, he thought. But he couldn't figure out how something as simple as wearing a tight costume would have helped, so he gave up on that line of reasoning and tried to come up with a better plan.

5

Cordelia brewed some tea in the hotel's kitchen, keeping an ear open for Wesley in the other room. She didn't expect to hear anything and her expectation was correct. He'd been remarkably quiet for the past hour or so. In her experience, a lot of people, maybe most, shifted and turned and moaned in their sleep, sometimes even breaking into soft laughter or frightened whimpers. Wesley, though, had been absolutely still for the longest time, so much so that she found herself watching his chest to make sure it continued to rise and fall with an easy rhythm. *As long as he breathes,* she thought, *he's okay. More or less.*

Alone with him in the silent hotel, though, she couldn't help thinking the worst. If he died, she just didn't know what she would do. She and Angel had already lost Doyle, and that was hard enough. But she and Wesley went back farther than she and Doyle, all the way back to Sunnydale, when he had arrived from England, sent by the Watcher's Council to replace Giles. He had been assigned to guide both Buffy and Faith, since Buffy's brief death and resurrection and the subsequent death of Kendra, Buffy's successor, had resulted in the two Slayers being active at the same time. Frankly, he hadn't been a huge success as a Watcher, Cordelia knew. He had redefined "stuffy," and both Buffy and Faith had seemed more than happy to completely ignore him, even though Cordelia had found him attractive.

Since he had shown up in Los Angeles, though, and become a full-fledged member of—then leader of—Angel Investigations, their relationship had taken a different course. They had grown ever closer, especially in those horrible days when Angel had gone on his Darla-inspired whirlwind tour of the dark side. There was nothing romantic now, nor would there ever be, Cordelia was sure. But they shared a kinship that was more like family than anything else she had ever known except perhaps for her connection with Angel himself.

And she wasn't just concerned for herself. Wesley had brought a different kind of leadership to the team. Angel's approach was direct and to the point— he was happiest if there was something he could go punch. But Wesley took a somewhat more cerebral look at an investigation, believing that going in with the fullest understanding possible, and then punching, would ultimately prove more effective. Angel had saved a lot of lives and helped a lot of people. But Wesley was building up a pretty good track record of his own, and the world would be a considerably darker, more frightening place without him in it.

She carried her tea back into the lobby and sipped it, standing beside Wesley's still form on the bed. *You have to come back to us,* she thought. *There's just no way around it. We need you. You have to come back.*

"And," she added aloud, "sooner is better."

6

"What is this?" the bouncer at the door demanded. He had to shout to be heard over the music that blared from within.

"It's a pass," Stanley Liebersoll insisted. Behind him, people were lined up waiting to pay their way and go inside, and for some reason this bouncer was questioning the validity of his pass. And the bouncer was about nine feet of solid muscle, with a head shaved as clean as a bowling ball and a Satanic goatee. His biceps were so big even the battleship tattooed on his left one looked small. Stanley was surprised the wooden bar stool he sat on didn't collapse beneath his weight. "I'm supposed to get in free."

The bouncer barked a sharp laugh. "Free? No one gets in free." He held up the pass. "That says 'Admit One;' it don't say nothing about free."

"But . . . the guy told me . . ."

"What guy?" the bouncer wanted to know.

"The guy who gave it to me."

"He work here?"

Stanley glanced back over his shoulder at the people waiting, less and less patiently, for him to get out of the way. "No," he said. "But he got it from someone who did. One of the, I don't know, promoters or something."

"First time I've ever heard that one," the bouncer said. "In the last five minutes or so, anyway. You get the name of this so-called promoter?"

"No," Stanley admitted. "He didn't say."

"The guy didn't say. Guy you got this from, who probably don't have a name either."

"He has a name," Stanley said. "It's Colin—"

"I'm sorry," the bouncer interrupted, his voice dripping with saccharine. "Did I accidentally give you the impression that I cared?"

"No," Stanley said. "You sure didn't." He wasn't getting past this guy for free, no matter what Colin had said.

"But you still want to go in?" the bouncer asked. "Even though you and I ain't going to become soulmates or anything?"

"I'd like to, yeah."

"Fifteen bucks," the bouncer said. He tore Stanley's pass into confetti-sized bits and let them fall to the ground, then put out a hand for the cash.

Stanley was tired of arguing, and the line of people behind him was getting vocal in their impatience. Fifteen dollars would buy a couple of loaves of bread, a gallon of milk, a jar of peanut butter, a

61

couple of boxes of macaroni and cheese, and then some, he knew. He would be giving up a lot to get into this club. But he'd already spent almost two hours getting down here on the bus, and he didn't have much money but he worked hard for what he had, and shouldn't a guy get to have some fun once in a while?

He dug out his wallet and forked over three fives, leaving him exactly one more until payday. The bouncer took the money and shoved it into a cigar box that was already full almost to overflowing and gave Stanley a broad, fake smile. A gold tooth glinted at the front of his mouth. "Have a good time," he said.

7

My name, Wesley thought, *is Wesley Wyndam-Pryce, and I don't belong here.*

There was only one possible answer. He was dreaming. If he was dreaming, then everything made sense—dream-sense, at any rate, which was an entirely different kind of sense altogether. The fact that he was down in the pit and knew what he was doing even though he'd never been in a mine in his life, could only work in dream-sense.

He had to get out. Or wake up. Preferably both.

He set down the double-pointed pick he'd been using to chip chunks of coal from the wall and picked up his lantern. Holding it close to his face, he approached the man he'd met, who had introduced himself as Rollie.

"I've decided that I don't belong here," he said. "I live in Los Angeles, California."

"You're a long way from home," Rollie said, sounding unconvinced.

"Take a good look at me," Wesley urged. "Have you ever seen me before?"

Rollie shook his head. "Means naught t'me, though. Plenty of boys come down pit to earn a few bob, then drift on t'the next one."

"I'm no coal miner," Wesley insisted. "I'm a detective. I work for Angel Investigations."

Rollie laughed, and Wesley saw that fully half his teeth were missing. "You look like a miner, not an angel," he said. "Or do they dress like us in California, as well?" Shaking his head again, Rollie returned to his work.

Wesley left him there and went back to the main shaft, carrying his lantern for what little good it did him. The main shaft was now populated almost solely by the occasional boy leading a pony, dragging tubs of coal behind it. But off the main shaft, Wesley realized, there were dozens of side shafts. In each of these, he heard the steady *chunk-chunk* of picks striking rock. Miners swore, their voices rough from the accumulated years of breathing in the coal dust. Some laughed and told jokes, a few sang songs, either steadily rhythmic in accompaniment to their work, or melancholy songs about girls with copper hair and eyes of blue walking in the sun.

In one of these shafts, Wesley saw a cage, and in the cage a small yellow bird, chirping merrily. *The canary*, he thought. *The proverbial canary in a coal mine.* If the air became too foul to breathe, too poisoned by methane, then the canary would die. As long as the canary lived, men could labor down here in the dark.

"'Aven't ye a place to work?" someone asked Wesley, anger tingeing his voice. "Ye're not gettin' paid t'wander about lookin' at birds and such, are ye?"

The man had a low, brutish brow over tiny eyes, almost as if his whole face were engaged in a defensive measure to protect vitals from the hazards of the underground world. A thick mustache drooped at the corners of his mouth, and a savage scar, black-edged, ran from just below his right eye to disappear under the end of the mustache. He fixed Wesley with a steady glare, lantern light glinting in those small, fierce eyes. "Yes," Wesley replied. "I do have a spot. I was just . . . stretching, a bit."

The miner let out a hard, barking laugh. "Stretching!" he echoed. "Well! Y'must be 'ere on 'oliday, then, eh?"

"No," Wesley said. He didn't know what else to say to the man, how to satisfy him, or even why he should. It wasn't as if he knew the fellow or would run into him in a pub after their shift in the mines was over. *I . . . I don't belong here, and I can't stay*, he thought. *I . . .*

But whatever thought had begun to form itself in his mind vanished just as fast as it had come. He turned away from the small-eyed man and made his way through the black pit, back to his station near the man named Rollie. The ceiling here was low, too low to stand upright. With back bent, Wesley returned to his work, forcing bits of coal from the stone with the end of his pick.

Midnight

1

Los Angeles International Airport—LAX, as it was known to most of the millions of travelers who passed through its doors every year—never really slept.

Its steady glow lit the night sky and could be seen from miles away, a patch of silvery luminescence on the ceiling of black. The glow came from lights at the parking structures, the runways, the terminal buildings—a small city's worth of lights, Angel thought. Jets flew in and out of the airport at all hours, and that meant that cars, buses, and trucks continually moved as well, into the parking structures and past the doors, up to the outlying private terminals. On the other side of the buildings, on and around the runways, the cars and trucks were joined by luggage haulers and fuel trucks and forklifts and security carts, each with its own headlights threading ribbons through the dark. Inside the terminal a skeleton crew worked the ticket counters. Janitors swept floors and polished rest rooms that were too busy to receive more than a cursory cleaning during the day. Security agents watched X-ray monitors and scanned the occasional passenger with a metal detector wand. Air traffic controllers drank coffee and sodas to keep their eyes open and their minds alert, so they could choreograph their delicate aerial ballet.

Angel parked the GTX in a nearly vacant customer parking area outside the UPX terminal. Most UPX branch offices were closed for the night, but the airport office, Angel knew, remained open twenty-four/seven. A neon UPX sign, in the traditional forest green and white, beamed from the office's front window. He hoped Gunn was making progress on the contact list, but his own efforts there would have to wait until he tried to track down the whereabouts of the truck that carried the Calynthia packages. He shrugged his shoulders, stood tall, and barged in through the glass doors, sweeping up to the package counter. A slight, bespectacled woman with graying hair and sleepy eyes looked at him. A name tag pinned to her striped sweater identified her as Emily.

"Can I help you?" she asked. Behind her, through an open doorway, Angel could see shelves and tables and rolling bins, and uniformed employees moving packages from one to another to a third. It all looked terribly random from here, but he knew there must be a finely tuned system behind it all.

"Detective Herb Saunders, L.A.P.D.," he lied, falling back on a tried and true pseudonym. "This is a police emergency." He hoped that impressing on her the urgency of his business would keep her from asking to see any identification, since he couldn't prove to be a police detective and he was sure she wouldn't help him if she knew he was a civilian.

"Oh, my," Emily said, her eyes widening.

"I need to locate a particular UPX truck," Angel went on. "It may have been involved in a crime. An ongoing crime. Can you do that?"

"We keep very close tabs on our vehicles," she said, sounding oddly proud. "We know where each one of them is assigned at any time. Do you know which truck it is that you're looking for?"

"RD-1472," Angel recited. He'd been standing with his face next to the truck's vehicle ID number until its back door had opened and the vamp had shot at him. "And as I said, it's an emergency, so the sooner you can track it the better."

Emily had been typing as he spoke, and when he was finished, she looked up at him and blinked behind her owlish glasses. "That's very strange," she said.

"What is?"

"That truck is in for service," she said. "It can't be involved in a crime—it's in the middle of a tune-up."

"Are you sure?" Angel asked her.

"That's what the computer says," she insisted.

"Can you double-check?"

"This is all quite exciting for me," she said. "You know, the graveyard shift is usually not all that thrilling. It's a lot of paperwork, some computer tracking, more paperwork. Day shift gets all the public contact, but this is time and a half so I do it."

"That's gotta be hard," Angel agreed, wishing she would move faster. "But you're providing invaluable help to an ongoing investigation, and I appreciate it."

She smiled a little and reached for a phone. Angel felt bad for her. This shift probably was a lonely one—no other customer had come in since he'd been here, and the people working in the back seemed too involved in their own tasks to interact with her. But that didn't mean he wanted to stand here and listen to the story of her life—particularly since the longer she talked, the more apt she was to ask him for some identification. And with Wesley's life in the balance, every second counted.

She had spoken a few sentences into the phone and then listened for a long time. Finally she thanked the person on the other end and hung up. "I'm surprised," she said.

"By what?"

"That you didn't already know. That truck was reported stolen this afternoon. Police officers have already been to the service yard and taken a report. Don't you people talk to each other?"

"Apparently not enough," Angel said. He knew that, depending on how many people had been targeted with the Calynthia attacks, there might be more than one truck involved. "Have any other trucks been stolen in the last day or so?"

"Let me check." Emily turned back to her computer for a moment, tapping on the keyboard and watching the monitor. "Oh, my," she said, surprised. "It's a regular crime wave. There have been four trucks stolen since yesterday."

Four UPX trucks. And it's entirely possible, Angel thought, *that other delivery companies have been hit as well. There's no telling how widespread this is.*

But it's bad, no doubt about that.

"Thanks for your help," he told her.

"Any time, Detective Saunders," she said. Angel was already heading for the door. "You come back and see me whenever you want. A little company helps the night go faster, you know?"

As far as Angel could tell, she might still have been talking to him as he drove out of the parking lot and away from the airport.

2

Gunn was having a lousy night.

He'd taken a cab back to where he'd parked the War Wagon, and then drove that truck, beast that it was, to the address that had been on the package Wesley had opened. *I really could use a Gunn-mobile. Or the power of flight. If I were a superhero, that'd be the one I'd want,* he thought. *Well, that and invulnerability.* As a kid, he'd always wanted X-ray vision, but he figured if he could fly and was invulnerable, the need for X-ray vision would be lessened, because the women would be pretty impressed with him as it was.

As Cordelia had reported, the address was nonexistent. It was on Sepulveda, which was about a thousand miles long, it seemed. But he found where it should have been, and the street numbers skipped right over it. As far as Gunn could tell, the precise address on the package was about halfway between a dry cleaner and a Shiatsu massage parlor, except that they butted up against each other in the middle of a block. The massage parlor, according to the pink neon sign in its window, was still open, but the dry cleaner had given up for the night. The rest of the block was taken up by a teacher's supply store, also closed, and a used car lot, ditto.

He started to head for the massage parlor's door,

but then changed his mind. Angel had suggested that somebody around here might have seen something. But there were no windows facing the street in that business except the front one, which was painted over except where the OPEN sign glowed, and that, it seemed, had a box behind it so there was still no seeing in or out. And it seemed like the kind of place where people would value their privacy—not likely that they'd tell him, even if they had seen anything. Besides, just because someone wrote an address down on a UPX label didn't mean they'd ever been in the neighborhood. He shrugged and went back to the truck, fishing the list Angel had given him from his pocket.

He tried the first address on the list. And the second. And the third. Each time, he found someone who had accepted and opened a UPX box full of the same green stuff that had knocked out Wesley. Each of the victims slept wherever they'd fallen.

Now he stood in front of the door to Madame LaTour's glamorous Coldwater Canyon home. He'd seen Madame LaTour's commercials on TV, advertising her psychic hotline service. The woman was, to put it bluntly, a babe and a half. She had a statuesque build, masses of velvety black hair piled on her head to make her look even taller, and clear green eyes—startlingly so, against the almost porcelain-like complexion of her skin—that almost made one believe she could see things others couldn't. He had never expected to meet her, and in fact had made fun of her claims on TV, even while admiring her striking appearance. But here he was.

And her door was ajar, which he took to be a very bad sign, because in this neighborhood nobody left the door ajar, especially not a famous and famously-beautiful woman like Madame LaTour. Not on purpose.

Gunn raised the heavy brass knocker and brought it down against its brass plate, three times, hard and fast. "Madame LaTour?" he shouted through the open door. There was no answer to that, either. He shivered, that bad feeling just getting worse and worse.

Her ornately carved wooden door was about three times the size of an average door—tall enough for a giant to enter, wide enough for a chariot to pass through. The whole house seemed like a fairy tale concoction, from what he could see spotlighted against the dark. Turrets reached into the sky, gables broke the roof line, ivy carpeted the walls. A floral fragrance drifted through the doorway, as if she had perfume piped throughout the house. When he pressed on the door, both hands flat against its elaborate surface, it felt like it weighed a ton—even more than it should have, given its large size.

When he had the door pushed open far enough to step inside, he discovered why.

Madame LaTour had collapsed just inside the

door, her body wedged against it. Next to her was a UPX package, and around her—smeared in an arc shape by the path she had taken as Gunn shoved the door open with her there—was the same green residue he'd seen on the other victims. *Too late again,* he thought. *Story of my life.* The TV psychic was just as lovely in repose as she had been on the screen, and Gunn felt tempted to straighten her out, since he'd kind of mashed her up against the wall by opening the door into her. But to do that would mean to touch her, and he couldn't risk becoming unconscious alongside her. Her diaphanous purple gown was dusted with residue from the package, and he couldn't see any place he could touch her that wouldn't be guaranteed to knock him out, stunningly inappropriate, or both. He simply left her where she was, sleeping soundly, and closed the door behind him.

3

On the dance floor, Blair was, to put it generously, a stiff. First of all, in spite of Jackie's urging that they stop at his place so he could change his clothes, he had declined, settling for taking off the tie and jacket he'd worn to dinner. Which meant that he was wearing an expensive linen shirt and suit pants and black leather loafers. She had taken his immaculate haircut into her own hands, mussing it as best she could, but it was so short that there really wasn't much to work with. Fortunately the place was dark and people were moving with such abandon, dancing and slamming and moshing, that it wasn't readily apparent that she was there with Mr. Straight.

The sad realization Jackie had come to, watching his earnest effort at dancing, was that the guy was just boring. And to Jackie, boring was the worst of all possible things to be. If she'd learned that he was an axe murderer, an embezzler, an international jewel thief—any of those things would have been a plus because they would have meant that the white-bread front he wore was a disguise, a boring cover hiding an interesting inside. But the more she got to know good old Blair, the more she realized that he was exactly who he seemed to be. He could hold up a conversation over dinner and he knew interesting people, but that didn't make him interesting himself.

Jackie put a great deal of emphasis on not being bored. She'd skated through high school—she was pretty, and guys had a tendency to want to help her with her homework, which smoothed things along to some degree, and she was smart enough to not need the homework to help her understand what it was they were trying to teach. Since graduating, she was taking some classes at UCLA, but not a full load and only late-afternoon classes. Daytime—like Blair—was boring. The sun could be counted on to come up every morning and shine most days. Sure, there were times when rain broke the pattern, sometimes for as many as three or four days in a row. But in Southern California, she had learned, one couldn't count on weather alone to keep things interesting. The sun was out, beaches and malls were crowded, freeways jammed. Jackie needed motion.

So she became nocturnal. In the dark of night, things happened. One could shop—the stores that were open were edgier, a little seedier, downright dangerous in some cases, but that just made them that much more fun. The beach was still there, though without the sun and the attendant crowds, so swimming was more of a challenge and skinny-dipping with friends was the way to do it. Streets flowed better late at night, the lights against darkness picking out the good bits and hiding the bland. And there were things to do at night: clubs, dances, parties, concerts, bars. A pretty girl could, with a little effort, get herself invited just about any place in town, and it didn't take long to learn who kept things jumping after the doors were locked and the civilians, the day-timers, sent home.

Jackie had started going to bed when the sun rose, then getting up at three or four unless she had a class she particularly wanted to make, spending a

leisurely "morning" at home, and then heading out
when the sun went down. Her parents had com-
plained, at first, but when they learned that they
weren't going to be able to change her, they settled
for her vague promises that she was careful and safe.

She knew the truth was that she was often neither
one of those things. The bigger truth was that it
didn't matter—those particular states of being were
not at all important to her. She was rarely bored—
that was what mattered.

But Blair, bless his lawyer's heart, was boring. He
was trying hard, and that counted for . . . well, nothing, really. He had a smile on his face, and sweat ran
down his cheeks and soaked through the chest of his
linen dress shirt. She moved close enough to him to
yell over the music.

"I think you should go now!" she shouted.

He looked perplexed, and stopped dancing.
"You're ready to leave?"

"Not me," she replied. "You!"

He touched his chest, and she nodded her assent.
"Yes. I'll stay a while longer, but you should go!"

"Why?" he asked.

"Because you don't like it here," she shouted.
"Not really. And I do."

"But . . . how would you get home?"

"I'll find a ride. It's not hard."

Blair shook his handsome head, and she saw how
out of place his classic looks were in this environ-

ment. She'd been eyeing a younger guy, with dark hair and smoldering eyes and a kind of dismissive sneer on his lips for a while, and now she realized that while he wasn't necessarily better looking than Blair, he was definitely more appropriate to the scene. "No," he said. "I'll stay as long as you do."

"No," she insisted. "If you stay, it's not with me."

"What does that mean?"

"It means I've had a great time. Well, an okay time. But it's over."

"Will I see you again?" he asked.

Jackie shrugged. "I don't think so. Around, maybe."

She didn't like the hurt look that crossed his face as the meaning of her words sank in. But she didn't hate it as much as being bored. Suddenly, though, the look changed, with one of anger replacing it. He grabbed her arm, hard.

"Come outside," he ordered her.

She yanked her arm away. It hurt where he'd held it. Now he was getting interesting, but it was too late for him. Nobody got more than one chance. "Why?"

"I want to talk to you," he shouted. "Where we can really talk."

She shook her head this time. "No need," she called back. "I've said all I'm going to." She turned away from him and went in search of the younger guy she'd spotted. Maybe he was worth getting to know.

4

Thirty minutes later Gunn walked into Connie's, an all-night coffee shop on Santa Monica where he had earlier arranged to meet up with some of his crew. He'd passed out portions of Angel's list to each of them, in order to cover still more ground in a timely fashion. Inside, the coffee shop was bright and pleasantly noisy, with orange Naugahyde booth benches occupied by a wide assortment of people— a gaggle of high school cheerleaders chattering in one, three solemn hip-hoppers sitting at another, spirits as low as if they were weighted down by their chains of gold, a young couple at still another sipping milkshakes as they spoke quietly of what seemed to be urgent issues.

Lightbulbs burned in fixtures shaped like wagon wheels, and paintings and wall carvings—desert landscapes, lonely cowboys, grazing cattle—continued the Western theme. The waitresses wore gingham dresses, paisley neckerchiefs, and ruffled aprons. Even the menus were decorated with cow-branding designs from famous cattle ranches in the Old West. Connie, for whom the place was named, had been Conrad Bell, a Western film star of the forties and fifties, and he'd built this coffee shop on prime Hollywood land in the heyday of his popularity. Since 1953, according to the sign on the door, the

joint had been open twenty-four hours a day, everyday. Gunn had read about a country-and-western
music star who'd gotten married here because he
liked the atmosphere and history. Gunn was no
country-and-western fan, but the food was good and
one could always count on the place being open.

The smells of coffee and grill food reached out to
Gunn, reminding him that he had been on the case
for hours. He spotted Chain, Rondell, and Rio in a
booth at the very back of the restaurant, as far from
the windows as they could get. They looked tired,
used up. Rio's eyes were barely open, and his chin
rested on his hands, which were spread flat on the
table. Empty cups and plates already littered the
laminated surface. Gunn acknowledged them and
sat next to Rondell, who moved over to let him onto
the bench. The waitress, a blond woman who looked
like she might have been a rodeo queen a couple of
decades earlier, appeared almost instantly, flashing
Gunn a bright smile and flipping open her order
pad. "Getcha something?" she asked cheerfully. *Too
cheerful,* Gunn thought, *for someone who's working
all night.*

"Coffee," Gunn said. "Lots of coffee. And apple
pie."

"Coming right up," the waitress said, disappearing on her rubber-soled shoes as quietly as she'd
come.

Gunn looked at the others. "Anything?" he asked.

"Man, that list you gave us, it's like an invitation to a party in the critical ward," Rondell said, shaking his head sadly. "Every single one of those people was already passed out, time we got around to them. You ever see the movie *Coma*? Now I know what it feels like to live it."

Chain passed Gunn a napkin rolled up around silverware. Gunn picked it up and tapped it a few times on the tabletop. "Same here," he said. "Whatever's going on, we're a step behind all the way."

"You ever gonna explain what's going on?" Rio asked, lifting his head off the table. "I mean, we could've been out hunting tonight, and instead you got us knocking on doors, looking at victims of some kinda nap dust. Maybe it's inconvenient for them, but it don't seem like life or death, know what I'm saying?"

"Soon as I find out what's goin' on, I'll explain it to y'all," Gunn said. "All I really know is that it's important. That some kinda big bad is goin' down, and the people who could best help prevent it are the people who are on the list. Which means, if we can't get to them before the bad guys do, then we just might lose this one. And also, a guy that saved my life might need me to do the same for him, if I can just figure out how to do it."

The others just looked at him, their faces empty of emotion. More and more, he knew, his fights weren't theirs, his concerns merited no more than passing curiosity on their part. Angel, Wesley, and Cordelia had saved all their lives more times than they could ever know, but he didn't try to fool himself that even that would carry any weight with them. They were focused on killing vamps. He had drilled the focus into them, and now it had become increasingly difficult to redirect their attention. Even though he now knew that, bad as vampires were, there were plenty of other things out there that were every bit as evil.

"We got any names left to check?" Gunn asked.

"A few," Chain said. "Out in the Valley, Orange County, one over in Redlands. Long drives for something that ain't even our business."

"Depending on what's really happening," Gunn argued, "it might be our business. We're in the dark, so far, but whatever is shakin', it's not small-time. Judging from their target list, I'd guess this is something that's going to affect everyone. The whole city, the state. Maybe more." He searched their faces. *They're not buying,* he thought. *Time for the secret weapon.* Angel had called him on his cell phone earlier, after the encounter with the UPX truck, to warn him about what they were dealing with. "And the guys doing this? They're vamps."

A wide smile crossed Rio's face, and he finally looked awake. "Give me that list," he said.

5

"I'm telling you, man, that was Angel."

Lenny nodded, keeping his hands on the wheel and his eyes on the road, though every now and then they ticked toward the mirrors, as if checking for pursuit. "I'm not disagreeing with you, dude," Lenny said. "I just said maybe there was more than one vamp who'd attack us."

"And I say, have you ever heard of any other—any vamp that comes after his own kind—besides Angel?" Homer was shaken after the vampire's attack and his own response, kicking open the rear door and standing in the truck's cargo area shooting Calynthia-M at the guy. One sharp turn or sudden bump and he would have been the one eating pavement, instead of Angel.

"But if that was Angel, then the package you delivered to him didn't get to him."

"Or someone else opened it. I told you MacKenna should have put his full name on it and not just the company name."

"I think MacKenna thought 'Investigations' was his last name," Lenny countered. He made a right turn onto a freeway on-ramp. "Anyway, I never heard of him even having a last name, have you?"

A short trip down the freeway would bring them to headquarters and a face-to-face with MacKenna that Homer was not looking forward to, not even a little bit. He could blame MacKenna's lack of preparation all night long, sitting here in the truck with Lenny, but when they told their boss that they'd missed Angel—and MacKenna insisted on hearing bad news in person, not over the phone—his wrath would be mighty indeed. *I'd rather tell him by postcard,* Homer thought. *From Pago Pago or someplace like that.*

He had once seen an enraged MacKenna tear a guy apart piece by piece with his bare hands—starting with his fingers and toes, waiting until he woke up every time he passed out before continuing, finally getting a doctor to drug him to keep him alert. That was the thing about vampires—they were so hard to kill that they could be tortured almost indefinitely, as long as the heart wasn't pierced by wood or the head removed. MacKenna had worked over this one vamp for three days before he got tired of it and threw him out into sunlight.

"You think we should have tried harder to get him when we saw him?" Lenny asked, as if remembering the same scene. Homer had pondered that same question but was hesitant to speak it out loud.

"Could be," he said. "But we did what we could, right? I don't know where he finally ended up hiding, but if we'd spent any more time on him we'd have missed half a dozen other deliveries."

"That's true," Lenny agreed. "Angel's important,

but you know what MacKenna said. Anyone on his list could interfere—they all have to be taken out, not just some of them."

"Let's just hope he remembers that," Homer said. At this point, speeding toward home, facing MacKenna was starting to look more frightening than facing Angel had been.

6

Tap-tap.

Tap-tap.

Wesley put his pick down for a moment, head on the ground, handle held loosely in his fist, his palm burning now with blisters from the labor. His back screamed with pain from working hunched over; his head throbbed from trying to see in the faint light and from breathing the foul air.

Tap-tap.

There it is again, he thought. *I knew I'd heard something.*

By now, he was used to the noises that the picks made *chunking* into the rock walls after coal, and this sound was nothing like those. It was an isolated, soft tapping that seemed to have no particular source but to come from all around him. The rhythm reminded him of a doctor tapping on a knee with a reflex hammer: a quick double-tap, then a pause, then a repeat.

Nothing he'd seen down in the mine would account for what he was hearing.

He picked up his lantern and went looking for Rollie, who had been working up the shaft a ways. He found the man sitting and eating lunch with another miner. Both had careful grips on their pasties, which had breading at the edges that served as handles so the miners could eat the centers without touching their meal with their filthy hands. Rollie laughed when he saw Wesley approach.

"You're still wi' us? Haven't gone back to California?"

"I'm still here," Wesley admitted wearily.

Rollie nudged the other miner with his clogged foot. "This one says he don't belong down pit, but home in California."

The other miner snickered. "'Ow'd you get 'ere, then, boy? They got a train now, from there?" His accent was different from Rollie's. Welsh, Wesley guessed.

Wesley ignored their jibes. "I heard a strange noise," he said. "Like a tapping sound. Tap-tap, then a pause, and then another tap-tap. It repeated over and over. Do you gents know what that is?"

The Welsh miner shuddered, and in the dim light from the lanterns, Wesley thought he saw a cloud of fear pass over the man's face. "Tommyknockers," the miner said.

"Excuse me?"

"Dafydd's from Wales," Rollie explained. "They've a story that there're little people live down in the mines. When there's goin' t'be a cave-in, then the tommyknockers tap on the beams and rafters t'warn the miners."

"Saved me da's life, they did," Dafydd explained. "'E 'eard the tommyknockers and got out just in time."

A miner's tall tale, Wesley thought. *The Welshman certainly seems to believe, but Rollie is obviously not concerned.* He thanked the men and went back to his work spot, where he'd left his pick and the tin that contained his own lunch—a tin that Wesley now remembered, somewhat uncomfortably, was called a Tommy tin. He was hungry; in fact he was famished now that he thought about it. Even a pastie sounded good. He'd taken drinks from his pocket flask now and again during the day, surprised to find that it was tea instead of water, but he hadn't opened the Tommy tin yet to see what food he had with him.

As he sat to open the tin, the years faded away and he remembered where he'd heard the tommy-knockers story before. His grandfather had told him about the mine-dwelling fairies when Wesley was a boy visiting his mother's father at his home in Cornwall. Wesley's great-grandfather had been a coal miner, as had the men of several generations before him. Wesley's grandfather was the first male of the family in decades who had avoided the mining life. He had delighted in telling stories of fairies and pixies and elves, and tommyknockers had been one of his standards because of his own father's time in the mines.

There had been another story he used to tell about the mines too, but Wesley couldn't quite bring it into focus in his mind. He remembered sitting on his grandfather's lap, feeling the old man's rough, weathered hands and cheeks. He always started with the tommyknockers story and then moved into the other one, Wesley knew. But try as he might, he could not remember what the second mining story had been about.

7

Cordelia turned away from the computer and rubbed her eyes. She had been at it for too long, following link after link, reading anything related to sleeping potions, which had then led to a side search on sleep disorders. She thought narcolepsy sounded promising. Maybe they were barking up the wrong tree—maybe Wesley suffered from the debilitating sleeping sickness, and whatever the mystery substance was had simply set off an attack. She found that it was rarely diagnosed correctly until years, sometimes decades, after symptoms set in, and that one person in every two thousand suffered from it. Reading about the disease, which caused excessive sleepiness and sometimes sudden, uncontrollable sleeping incidents, she even began to wonder about herself. *I'm always sleepy,* she thought. *But then, working with a vampire means a lot of late or sleepless nights, followed way too often by sleepless days, too. So some fatigue isn't surprising. Plus, unsightly puffiness around the eyes is probably more a symptom of knowing Angel than of narcolepsy.*

Cordy had already read about and discarded a dozen other possibilities. *The green mist didn't look like Chamomile,* she thought, which was one of the common ingredients in Wiccan sleep spells. Rising to glance at Wesley, still unmoving in the bed, she knew that she had to keep looking, that there had to be some way to help him and she needed to find it, no matter how difficult it was. She returned to the keyboard and followed another link.

This one took her to a collection of stories and legends about sleep—old wives' tales, she figured, like the one about the man whose snoring drove his wife to sleep out in the backyard, giving her pneumonia. That one, according to the site, wasn't true, though it detailed a number of factual snoring incidents, and gave some possible solutions to snoring problems. But that didn't help Cordelia—Wesley was barely breathing audibly, and a long way from snoring. So she continued down the line of folk tales, eventually finding some that sent a chill down her spine.

Another story she had always dismissed as a myth was the one about people dying in their dreams, causing their real-life deaths. She was pretty sure she'd died in dreams before, but she was still here. But reading further, she found that there was another factor she had never considered. One that definitely seemed to be in play here.

Magick.

If the sleep, she discovered, was somehow magickally induced, via a sleeping potion or spell, then events in dreams could, in fact, have consequences in the real world. In one case, a woman who dreamed that her legs were broken in a car accident— after she'd put herself to sleep using a potion she'd purchased from a Chinese wizard—had awakened to find that both of her legs had become paralyzed. Doctors examining her found no medical explanation for the paralysis, but she had had to go through months of agonizing physical therapy to retrain her muscles before she could walk again. There was no direct evidence that one could die due to dying in a dream, probably because anyone who never woke up wouldn't be in a position to report what they'd been dreaming about. But the inference was made, just the same.

Cordelia had been worried about Wesley before, but now her emotional pendulum swung back toward panic. *Who knows what he's dreaming about?* she thought. Considering the way he went to sleep, an innocent victim of an exploding box, chances were he could be having some pretty serious nightmares. She did from time to time, after encounters with particularly unpleasant demons and beasties.

He's just got to wake up, she thought. *That's all there is to it.*

She left the desk and went to him. He looked so peaceful there, his lips parted slightly as air passed in and out, his eyes gently shut. He looked calm, at rest. She almost envied him, since it didn't look like she'd be getting much sleep tonight.

"Wesley," she said, hopefully. "Wesley? It's time to wake up, now. You've had a nice little nap, but now it's over. Come on, Wes. Come and see Cordelia."

He didn't stir.

"There are women here to see you, Wes. Beautiful ones. Dancers with long legs. They came to meet you."

Still nothing.

"I'll go see an English movie with you if you'll wake up, Wes. One of those incredibly boring Merchant/Ivory films, based on a novel by some long-dead Englishwoman. Sound good? I'll even treat."

He breathed softly, in and out. She thought one eye twitched a little. *Probably the "I'll treat" line,* she thought. *That would get a reaction out of him, even if nothing else did.*

Obviously, talking wasn't doing the job. She put a hand on his shoulder and gently shook him. His breathing caught for a second, but then it settled back into its normal rhythm. She shook him harder. No reaction at all. She took his arm and wrenched it, yanking him so hard she almost pulled him from the bed, then shoving him back the other way. "Wake up!" she screamed as she tugged on him. "Wesley, wake up!"

When she let him go, his eyes twitched, both of them fluttering a couple of times, but he immediately sank back into his deep sleep.

"Oh, wake up already," she moaned, frustration hitting her like a football tackle. She went back to the computer, where at least tapping on the keys might lead to some sort of quantifiable results.

One O'Clock

1

Wesley felt himself being shaken by some external force. In the dark, he couldn't see what it was—his first thought was that it was just another Southern California earthquake, but just as suddenly he forgot how he'd ever have experienced Southern California earthquakes. He heard noises all around him, though, a steady, insistent rumbling, and a sound like a driving rainfall. Then bits of rock started hitting him, dropping from the invisible ceiling above. A larger chunk glanced off his cheek, and he raised a blackened hand to it. His fingers came away wet, glistening with what looked, in his lantern-light, like a deeper black. He was bleeding.

He ducked his head as the mineral rain came harder and faster, the chunks getting bigger and more dangerous.

Then he heard Rollie scream. "Cave-in!" the man bellowed. "Cave-in!"

Snatching up his lantern, Wesley ran for where the other miner had been working. The ground shook beneath his feet, and he was unsteady on his strange metal-soled clogs to begin with. He felt himself falling—he could have been in free fall for all he knew, since the ground, the roof, and the walls were all submerged in pitch black, making them invisible. The ground was there, though, and he hit it hard, hands splayed out to either side. His face smashed into the rocky floor. Bright flashes of light disoriented him until he realized they were just impact bursts. When he regained his balance on his hands and knees, he realized he was completely in the dark—his lantern had gone out or rolled into a crevice somewhere. Wesley pawed the ground around him, panic rising in his throat.

Even as he searched for the small solace of light, the rumble grew to a deafening roar. Dust filled the air, gagging him, and he fell back to a sitting position, shutting his mouth and eyes against it. The thunderous noise echoed for a while, and longer in Wesley's ears, which rang from the power of it. When he could hear clearly again, he realized that it had become very quiet, with only the rattle of a few falling stones breaking the silence. He found his lantern then, its flame extinct, the metal already cooling. His first thought was to strike a match, but he quickly discarded that notion. If the cave-in had released more methane into the air, lighting a flame would be the surest way to make sure he didn't survive the experience. Even the coal dust choking the shaft could be explosive. After all, coal was for burning.

At least I'm alive, he told himself. *There's been a cave-in, but I'm alive. That's something, isn't it?*

He was lost in the bowels of the Earth, in absolute pitch black, all alone. It seemed unlikely that anyone would care that he was down here, because he couldn't think of anyone who would be on the surface waiting for him. He had a numbered lantern, so they'd know he was missing. But who was up there in the sunlight? Who would be pacing a wooden floor, waiting for news, or standing vigil for him outside the pit? He tried to recall names or faces of people who might care where he was, but he couldn't. The faces floated just out of sight, obscured as if behind a veil or on the other side of a window on a rainy day. *Surely there's someone,* he thought. *Someone who cares if I live or die down here in the dark.*

Though for the life of me, I can't imagine who.

ANGEL

2

The side of the building that faced onto Rosecrans,
in the community of Downey, looked like a warehouse with rust-pocked corrugated metal walls,
most of which had been pasted over by years and
years' worth of posters and handbills advertising
everything from concerts and movies to sales on car-
pet remnants or auctioned cars. But what looked
like a quiet warehouse was actually an after-hours
rave club that did a booming business most nights,
drawing in young people from dozens of miles in
every direction for a night of ferociously loud music,
shouted conversation, dancing, and general merri-
ment of which their parents would no doubt disap-
prove. Cars came and went all night, every night,
but during the day the place was still and empty.

That was just how MacKenna liked it, with the
sleeping during the day thing and all. At night, when
the club was rocking, he was awake anyway. The
constant traffic of vehicles and people covered his
own comings and goings at night—as well as providing the occasional meal. And the din from the dance
floor always drowned out any screams that might be
associated with his dining.

MacKenna had set up headquarters in the back of
the club, using a separate VIP entrance so he and
his people didn't have to fight through the throngs

96

on the dance floor to get in or out. In this neighbor-hood, which otherwise closed down completely when dark descended over the city, finding the space attached to the club had been a stroke of luck or genius. MacKenna, of course, would claim the latter, but Homer wasn't so sure. He worked for MacKenna—more and more of L.A.'s vampires seemed to work for MacKenna, since MacKenna always seemed to have some coin to pay with and some meat to play with, and weren't those two things really the keys to a happy un-life?

Homer had been a solo act for most of the three decades or so since he'd been made, back in rural North Carolina. He'd lived near the Great Dismal Swamp. His daddy had hunted in the swamp and run a gas station, and Homer had hunted in the swamp and worked for Daddy, figuring that one day he'd inherit the gas station. If it wasn't the most glamorous life, well, at least it was a good thing for a man to know what he was doing and where he was going.

But then one night he'd been sitting with his feet up on a milk can, chair tipped back, head against the outside wall of the station, when a long red car had pulled up to the pump. Inside the car was a woman with lips that matched the car and hair almost as red, and big blue eyes that burned into Homer when she looked at him. "I'm afraid I've lost my way," she said. "Could you possibly direct me to the highway?"

Well, Homer could direct her anywhere in the county, but he knew that there was no highway within a dozen miles, so she was either more lost than she thought or she was pulling his leg. His daddy wasn't around, so he decided to pull back. "Which one, ma'am?" he asked her. "The highway to New York? The one to Atlanta, maybe? How about the one to Paris, France?"

She laughed as if he were a comedic genius, maybe one of those people on *Laugh-In* or something. "You're teasing me," she said, and her cheeks went a pleasing shade of pink. But she was smiling and he could tell she wasn't really complaining. "Stop it."

He had kept on, though, and finally she had begun laughing right out loud. When she was able to bring herself under control, she told Homer that she was hungry. He explained to her that the candy machine was out of order and the store shut for the night, so she'd have a ways to go if she wanted something to eat. But she just kept looking at him, her eyes holding his, and she shook her head slowly. "No," she said. "I don't want to wait at all." Then she'd brought her mouth to his neck, and his first thought was that he was going to have some story to tell the guys tomorrow—until he felt her teeth sink into his throat.

She didn't kill him, though. She turned him and then took him along with her in her big red car.

After he had come to and she'd introduced him to the glories of eternal undeath, she explained that she'd been targeted by a squad of vampire killers hired by a small community up near Richmond, so had needed a quick escape and a good hiding place. The Great Dismal Swamp seemed like it'd do, but she needed a native guide, someone who knew the lay of the land. That's where Homer came in. He kept her safe there for a couple of weeks while she made arrangements to move out of the area altogether. He had never seen her again after that, though he'd wandered the country looking for her. Every now and then he heard rumors about her, and one of those had brought him to Los Angeles, where he'd fallen in with MacKenna.

Her name had been Dinah, and he'd always love her.

Lenny interrupted Homer's reverie by bringing the stolen UPX truck to a shuddering stop up against one of the warehouse's side walls, between an ancient primer gray Econoline van and a shiny red Acura NSX. Children of L.A.'s rich and poor mingled here in a way they didn't in almost any other facet of their lives.

"We got to get rid of this truck pretty soon," Homer reminded him. "Cops'll be looking for it already."

Lenny nodded as if he was perturbed that Homer was even bringing it up. "I know, man," he replied.

"It's got numbers and stuff all over it; it ain't like it's invisible."

Earlier in the day Homer had almost felt like it *was* invisible because it was so ubiquitous. People saw UPX trucks so often they forgot to even notice them. *Like one-dollar bills,* he thought, *or long-distance ads.* But as the night wore on, there were fewer of them on the streets, and at some point it would become a flashing beacon calling attention to itself.

They sat silently in the dark for a moment as a young couple passed the truck without a second look. The boy wore pants that four of himself could have fit into, a tight black mesh tank top, leather fingerless gloves, copious amounts of metal hanging around his neck and impaling various bodily features, and heavy black shoes with the laces untied. The spikes of his Day-Glo green hair reached almost nine inches above his head. His female counterpart was dressed in a girl's school uniform with pleated plaid skirt, white kneesocks and saddle shoes—if there were a girl's school where the uniform included a leather corset that cinched her waist under the bustline, and a leather collar studded with half-inch metal spikes. Her hair, in shades of pink and purple, was pulled back into braided pigtails, each tied at the end with a strip of plaid ribbon from which hung tiny plastic skulls.

Watching them walk by, Homer turned to Lenny and spoke quietly. "And people think *we* look weird."

When the street was clear, they got out of the truck and headed for the building's rear entrance. Homer was nervous. MacKenna didn't respond well to bad news, and worse to failure. Homer couldn't keep his mind off the rumor that MacKenna had once made a habit of chaining those who displeased him to mule-drawn carts sent—slowly—in four different directions, in order to watch their faces as they were pulled apart. If there were any mules in twenty-first century Los Angeles, Homer didn't know about them, but MacKenna could have modernized his methods to keep with the times. *And I don't even want to think about that.*

Inside this end of the building, the space looked like the abandoned warehouse that it was. The door opened onto a vast, cavernous room dimly lit by bare lightbulbs hung high up in the rafters. This room was only a smokescreen, though—the real action took place down below the cement floor. An opening in the floor that looked like a mechanic's pit actually opened onto a doorway that led down a flight of stairs to a large underground area. Guards stationed in the rafters, above the lights, were surely watching Homer and Lenny as they walked through the near dark, down the short flight of steps into the pit, and opened the door that hid the inner stairs. Any human who wandered in here would already have been meat.

"Just let me do the talking," Homer whispered as they started down.

"Hey, that's fine with me, man," Lenny replied. "You talk all you want. I'll just hang in the background."

The space under the earth was nearly as large as the warehouse had been. The light here came from candles, hundreds of them burning all at once, sending streamers of smoke and pungent odors into the air. Several dozen vampires were already in the space, lounging on pillows or sofas, leaning against the wall and muttering softly to one another, or snacking on humans they had captured. More streamed in as Homer looked around. He heard sucking sounds from dark corners and the sad whimpers of one of the victims who had not yet lost consciousness. The smell of blood was everywhere down here, battling for primacy with the scents of the candles.

At the end of the room MacKenna sat in his big chair. Homer thought it was uncomfortably similar to a throne, and that MacKenna fancied himself a king. But if anyone had a right to, he supposed MacKenna was the guy. He had united Southern California's vampire community in a way that no one else had managed since the Slayer had killed the Master. From this base in Los Angeles his tendrils reached to San Diego and the Inland Empire, and he seemed to have connections even in Sunnydale.

And if his current scheme worked, vampires everywhere would have reason to know his name and sing his praises.

He spotted Homer and Lenny as they made their way across the room toward him, and a grin appeared on his handsome face.

"Homer, Lenny," he said cheerfully, patting down his bright red hair as if to make himself look more presentable for company. "Welcome, my friends. Come on in, make yourselves comfortable. Can we get you a bite to eat?"

MacKenna was powerfully built, and his white dress shirt was open to the waist, exposing his muscled chest and washboard stomach. Over the shirt was a black leather jacket that hugged his shoulders and arms. Black leather pants and shiny boots completed his ensemble.

"No," Homer said. "Thank you, anyway. We're not here to stay long."

MacKenna looked crestfallen at this news. "You're not? But why? Surely you're finished with your mission."

Homer swallowed. This was the hard part, especially in front of so many of his fellows. "Well, not completely," he said. "We delivered all the packages—"

"Grand," MacKenna interrupted. "That's excellent."

"—but one of them didn't quite make it to the target."

MacKenna's face clouded over. The vampire made no attempt to disguise his moods, but allowed them to show on his face as plainly as if they'd been written there. Homer always believed it was a sign of MacKenna's power—he could afford to let people know what he was thinking, because he could back up his will with strength.

"The others have all reported back," the head vamp said, sounding disappointed. "All over the city, people are sleeping—occultists, magicians, metaphysicians, astrologers, astronomers, rocket scientists. A wide cross-section, wouldn't you agree, of Los Angeles denizens. Carefully researched and targeted, because they are the people—well, people and, in some cases, demons—who could possibly prevent our little operation from succeeding tonight. And may I remind you, if it doesn't succeed now we'll be waiting several hundred years for the time to come around again. But you—Homer, Lenny, two of my very favorites—you tell me one of your targets was missed?" He put a finger to his lips, almost daintily. "I wonder if I might ask who."

"It's his fault," Lenny said nervously, jabbing a thumb at Homer. "I mean, I was just driving the truck. He was the one who went inside and delivered all the packages and everything, you know?"

"Hey!" Homer objected.

TRANGER TO THE SUN

"Lenny, Lenny, I'm not finding fault here," MacKenna put in. "It's just that if there's a hole in the plan, I want to know what it is. So tell me, who got left out? Some aged engineer? A lonely numerologist, perhaps?"

"No," Homer said. "It was Angel, okay? Angel."

A look of concern flashed across MacKenna's face, and several of the other vamps in the room groaned or audibly swore. "L.A.'s own self-hating, holier-than-thou prima donna vampire?" MacKenna asked. "That Angel?"

"I delivered the package to Angel Investigations, but one of the other people there accepted it. I guess they must have opened it without waiting for Angel or something."

"And you know this how?" MacKenna followed up. "You waited around to observe, maybe?"

"He kind of attacked us, later on," Homer admitted. "He came at the truck. We held him off with more of your concentrated Calynthia-M, but we couldn't tag him with it."

"So did he follow you here, do you think?" MacKenna asked casually.

"No way," Lenny said. "I was driving. No one followed us, I made sure of that."

"It sounds," MacKenna said, "like you did everything right, Lenny. While Homer fouled up again and again."

"That's pretty much right," Lenny said.

"And Angel remains a threat to us," MacKenna observed. "So you won't mind if I put you in charge now, Lenny. You and Homer can go find Angel—and finish him. And if you fail to do so, well then, I'll hold you responsible, Lenny. Since you did everything so right."

Homer stole a glance at Lenny's face, enjoying the look of horror that painted itself there. "I can live with that," Homer said.

"Uhh . . . I . . . I guess if . . . if that's what you w-want," Lenny stammered.

"It is," MacKenna confirmed. "As for the rest of you, I don't need to explain to you again, I hope, why tonight is the only night for the next three hundred and thirty years that this will work. Now that Angel is aware that something's up, he'll be looking for us. He may be a traitor to our kind, but he's smart. Let's not forget that. Everyone be on your guard, and if you see him, kill him.

"Unless, of course, Lenny kills him first."

Homer almost felt bad for his partner. If they didn't bring Angel in, then he'd suffer some kind of humiliation, but Lenny would suffer more. His humiliation would be painful—and fatal.

MacKenna dismissed them, waving them away with both hands. "Go, go. There's much to do!"

On the way back to the stairs, Homer just couldn't resist one more dig. "I told you to let me do the talking."

3

UPX worked all through the night, using the hours when the rest of the world slept to process and move packages from coast to coast. Since they were on the move all night, their trucks had to be serviced at all hours. There were three service yards in the greater Los Angeles area to take care of them. Angel drove to the one from which the truck he'd spotted earlier had been stolen, in Glendale.

The yard was bathed in bright light from tall lamps mounted on poles, and more bulbs scattered around the service bays. There were, Angel guessed, a dozen people working, mostly mechanics in grease-stained coveralls crawling inside and under the trucks and vans that carried packages.

One of them, a heavyset guy with a mop of dark curly hair and round cheeks, grabbed a clipboard off a counter and approached Angel as he wandered into the yard. The name tag sewn onto his coveralls said "Chad." "Help you?" he asked, a friendly note in his voice.

"I'm looking for information about a truck that was stolen from here today," Angel replied.

"I think the day crew already talked to the cops about it."

"Probably they did," Angel said. "But I think it's a little more complicated than the cops know about."

"What do you mean?" Chad asked. "Complicated? Like, a federal matter? Organized crime?"

Angel nodded. "Along those lines."

"Geez," the guy said, and gave a low whistle. "I didn't think it was anything like that. Maybe kids out for a joyride or something."

"We only wish," Angel said. He'd learned long ago that most people, especially those working at night, were happy to talk about their jobs and their lives with anyone who showed an interest. And they were even quicker to talk if he could make what they did seem like it was important to him.

Chad crooked a finger and led Angel to a parking area near the tall fence that surrounded the yard. "It was sitting right back here," Chad said. "Let's see, it was RD . . ."

"RD-1472," Angel finished. He knew the guy was testing him.

"That's right," Chad said. "It was waiting for its rotation into the bay. Basic maintenance, tune-up, lube. All the usual checks and balances, you know?" He chuckled at that. "Checks and balances, get it?"

"Got it."

"Come on," Chad said, leading Angel away from the lot toward the main building in the center of everything. "Here's the weird thing."

"What's weird?" Angel asked.

They passed through a glass door and walked inside

the seemingly empty building. Chad put his clipboard down on the front counter and moved behind the counter, where he removed another clipboard from a slot in the wall. He carried this clipboard back to the counter and set it down in front of Angel. "Every vehicle in or out has to be signed in or out. We don't just let 'em drive around, you know?"

"Makes sense."

"So this one, it was signed in day before yesterday. Well, now that it's past midnight and today is today instead of tomorrow . . . or yesterday, if you see what I mean."

"It was signed in the day before it was stolen," Angel said.

"Yeah, that's it. Its regular driver, Glen Murphy, brought it in, signed it over to us for the service. Then he took off. Here's his signature, see?"

Angel looked at it. The handwriting was a scrawl, but it could have said Glen Murphy.

"Then yesterday the truck was signed out again, before the service was even done. And it was signed out by Glen Murphy, see?"

Angel looked. The scrawl was similar to the first. *Not identical*, he thought, *but rarely does anyone sign their name in absolutely identical fashion time after time. These are pretty close.* He pulled the clipboard over and looked again. They were *very* close. The swoop of the *G*, the loop of the *l*, the double hump of the *M*, were all identical.

"It's a good forgery," he said.

"It's a forgery?" Chad asked, sounding surprised.

"That'd be my guess," Angel told him. "The various parts of the name that anyone would look at—anyone who wasn't an expert, anyway—are all perfect. Like they'd been practiced. But there are strange variations in the common letters in the middle of the names, the way the *u* and the *r* join, for instance. See?"

"Way I heard it," Chad said, still skeptical, "they were pretty convinced it was Murphy. They tried to find him today, but he didn't answer his phone or his door. They think he came back, took out the truck, and took it someplace. Maybe he sold it, took the money, and left town. Something."

"And whoever accepted the truck and then let him leave with it—two different people, I'm guessing? Neither of whom knew Murphy?"

"The guy who checked the truck in was Evan, our day shift manager. He knows Murphy. But when Murphy or whoever came back for it, Evan was at lunch and Slott signed it out. He doesn't know Murphy from Adam. We have a couple thousand employees in the greater Los Angeles metropolitan region, you know? Said the guy had Murphy's ID and the signature looked right, so he handed over the keys, and Murphy or whoever it really was left with the truck."

Angel pushed the clipboard back to Chad. "I'll

need Murphy's address," he said. Chad looked hesitant, but then he shrugged and pulled a three-ring binder out from under the counter.

"You're in luck," he said. "We keep that information here, because if a driver forgets to pick up his truck, we need to be able to call him or someone else to take it off our hands. We can only accommodate so many trucks here. And UPX never sleeps, right?"

Angel smiled, watching Chad flip through the pages looking for the *M*s. "That's what I hear."

4

A huge parking lot surrounded the Los Angeles Herald building, but at this time of night, only the closest hundred or so spaces were filled. Gunn parked in the hundred-and-first space and crossed the floodlit lot to the front doors. He wasn't precisely sure how this was going to work, but he figured it was a pretty good idea, just the same.

Angel says this whole sleeping sickness thing is pretty widespread. I know the cops and paramedics are hearing about it; I gotta figure the press is hearing about it too. So here he was at one of L.A.'s biggest newspapers to see what he could find out about how many people were affected.

Just inside the front doors was a well-lit lobby with a security desk. The uniformed woman behind the counter gave him a smile as he came in. "What can I do for you?" she asked him.

He returned the smile. "I'm not really sure what I'm looking for," he said politely. "Maybe the city desk or the crime beat or something like that."

"Do you have a story to report?"

Do I ever, he thought, but of course he couldn't say that. "Mostly I'm looking for information, I guess."

"That's what we're all about," the guard said. Beyond her, through large windows, Gunn could see what he assumed was the press room or something. It was a huge space with row after row of desks, each with a computer on top, arranged like some giant checkerboard. But less than a quarter of the desks were occupied at this hour. At the rest, screens glowed but no one worked. "And in the morning it'll just cost you thirty-five cents to get some."

"The morning will be too late," Gunn said. "I gotta know now. I know it's a cliché, but it's kind of a matter of life and death."

"Oh, why didn't you say so?" the guard asked sweetly. "I'll show you right into our crank office with the rest of the lunatics."

Gunn seethed inwardly, but worked on maintaining control. He guessed the daytime guards were a little more diplomatic than this woman. *Maybe the reason she got stuck with the night shift,* he thought. "Look, I know this sounds crazy," he said. "Because I can't tell you how I know what I know or why I need to know what I don't know. But I know what I know, you know?"

The guard shook her head. "You lost me there. And you have about ten seconds to find me again before I throw you out."

"I know that there's been an epidemic of people falling asleep tonight. Knocked out by green dust or something. I even know what kind of people it's been happening to. People involved with the occult, with magick. Maybe people you'd put in your crank room."

The guard listened thoughtfully, nodded her head once, and then turned and picked up a telephone headset. She touched a couple of buttons on a control panel. "Jarod?" she said. "There's someone out here I think you should talk to."

5

"I can appreciate the skill of a good deejay," Jacquelyn Kirby was saying. "I mean, I've been dancing for two hours now, and this guy is awesome. I just don't see how you can call it an art."

While Stanley Liebersoll had noticed Jacquelyn

on the dance floor almost as soon as they got there, he had only met her a short while before. She had approached him and offered him a plastic water bottle. Eager to replenish what he had lost in sweat in the hot, crowded, noisy room, he had taken it with a smile and downed half the bottle, dancing as he did. Then he'd given it back to her and she'd finished it off without even wiping the bottle's mouth. They had been together ever since. Now they had decided to take a walk, to breathe in some fresh night air and actually be able to speak with one another in something more than hand signals for a while.

Stanley thought Jackie was the most lovely girl he'd ever seen. Her hair was jet black and cut close against her scalp, her eyes rimmed with black like an Egyptian princess of some kind, her left eyebrow pierced with three silver studs. Her outfit, all black and leather, included many zippers and studs and dangling chains. All in all, she seemed like the kind of girl a guy could spend a lifetime trying to get to know—just trying to find a way to meet, for that matter—and he was amazed that she'd shown any interest in him.

Yet here they were, three blocks from the club, wandering through a district of warehouses that were dark and empty at this time of night. And she was talking to him like she really cared about what he had to say. He thought this just might be the best night of his life. He felt like he wanted this night to go on forever, because if the sun ever rose then she might vanish, pull a Cinderella and run away with the strokes of the clock or simply fade in the first rays of the sun. If she was a dream or an illusion he never wanted to wake up, to face reality. Stanley considered himself a child of the night, and looking at Jackie, it was clear to him that she was the same, and there was no telling what flaws the sun's harsh light would expose on either one of them.

"It's like any artist," he said at length. "A painter, a sculptor, a musician, whatever. What do they do? They take some kind of raw material, be it paint, be it marble, be it snatches of music they hear in their own brains, and they shape it into something different, give it some kind of order, of form. Even if it's formless form, you know? It's passed through them and becomes something else. That's what a good deejay does. It's just that his raw materials are recordings that someone else has made. Doesn't mean he's not making new art with them."

She stopped and studied him for a moment, her tongue flicking across her lips and exposing the silver ball near its end. The simple motion made him quiver, almost melt. "I suppose, when you put it that way," she said. "That makes a certain amount of sense."

Stanley exhaled. He had been holding his breath to see if he could manage to convince her of his point of view in their first real conversation. If he'd been unable to sway her, he'd have figured this connection probably wasn't worth taking any farther. But since he'd been successful in this, maybe she'd be amenable to more persuasion down the line. He had to try, even if it was premature. There were hours of darkness yet to share, and he was pushing his luck but he couldn't resist.

"So, uh . . . you want to try to get together sometime during the week?" he asked her nervously. "Maybe go out, have some fun or something?"

She never got a chance to answer.

The shadows around them came alive, arms reaching out toward them. Jackie started to scream, but a hand clamped over her mouth and cut her off. Before Stanley could make a move toward her there was another one on him, powerful arms snaking around his neck and chest and pulling him close. The creature had a strange protruding forehead with deep furrows, beady pale eyes, and long, sharp-looking fangs. When it spoke, its voice was a sibilant whisper, and its foul breath washed across Stanley like a sewer being opened. "Shhh. Not a word, now," it said. "You kids are coming with us."

Two O'Clock

1

MacKenna paced the floor of the big room as his acolytes laid down the correct markings on the stone. He was worried about tonight. It had to go right—*had* to. There was no second chance here. No "do-overs." Tonight was the real thing, the main event, and when the morning came—for some, anyway—everything would be different.

"You there!" he shouted to an acolyte whose line was wavering a little. "Careful. Straighter! This has to be perfect!"

The acolyte glanced up in terror—which was the reaction MacKenna had been hoping for, the reaction he drilled into his followers—and resumed his work, being more precise about it now. Precision counted, with a spell as complex as MacKenna had planned for many years.

Padraic MacKenna had emigrated to the United States in 1846, after the failure of the potato crop in Ireland had spurred a nationwide famine there. Like most Irish immigrants he had landed in New York. After a few weeks looking for work, the young man, just seventeen at the time, fell in with a gang of toughs on the Lower East Side, and quickly found that a good income could be had for a young man with ready fists and little conscience. He rose rapidly in the ranks of the gang, his skill and aptitude for violence making him an indispensable asset to the organization.

A few years later, though, he found that the atmosphere in New York was becoming hazardous to his health. The sons of the recently deceased leader of a rival gang had some issues they wanted to discuss with Padraic MacKenna, and their discussion would likely end with MacKenna's lifeless corpse floating in the East River. Hoping to avoid such a conversation, MacKenna took a train west, eventually disembarking in San Antonio, Texas. A telegraph message had gone ahead of him, and he was met at the station by a few friends and associates who had preceded him to the frontier.

The West was a very different place from New York. But New York had been different from

Ireland, and Padraic MacKenna was a man who adapted well to changing circumstances. As before, he assimilated fast, soon becoming an expert rider. Here, as back in New York, he was able to put his particular combination of brutal violence and lack of compassion to good use. His new gang, an amalgamation of both Irish and non-Irish fellows, robbed the occasional bank when times were hard, but their real specialties were mail and train robberies. These sorts of jobs took place on the move instead of in fixed locations, so there was less risk of capture by local authorities. And lawmen, it turned out, liked to stay in town when they could, so by pulling their jobs far from town, the gang usually enjoyed a healthy head start. MacKenna began to like this western life, riding fast and living large under wide-open skies.

It was after a particularly successful train robbery, during which they had taken the payroll for a large mining outfit, that Padraic MacKenna's life had changed forever.

Escaping from the train, they had ridden hard for the border, finally coming to rest in Matamoros, Mexico to spend some time and money while the heat died down. MacKenna and the boys passed their days sleeping and their nights playing cards and drinking expensive whiskey in some of Matamoros's most exclusive saloons. Which, as it turned out, wasn't saying much, as the dusty border town's idea of high class meant planks had been laid over the dirt floors, and the barkeep sometimes used water when washing out the glasses between customers.

But on their third night there MacKenna had his attention grabbed by a beauty with flashing dark eyes, raven hair, and olive skin that set off her even, white teeth beautifully. They made eye contact in the saloon, and he started toward her only to have her slip out the door into the night. He followed. Outside, he looked in both directions down the town's broad main street, but she was nowhere to be seen. So he turned off the main street, onto the side roads that quickly became a maze of narrow alleys and seemingly haphazard structures. He heard running footsteps from time to time, though, and occasionally caught a glimpse of her flowing tresses at the end of a street. He knew he was being played, but it only made him more determined to find her.

Finally, spotting a darting shadow on an alley wall, he sprinted hard and came upon her, leaning against a barrel on the road and laughing. Her long dark hair was mussed, her skirts ruffled, and her laugh was as carefree and honest as any sound MacKenna had ever heard. When she was able to speak, she did so in heavily-accented English. "You caught me," she said, catching her breath. "So I am your prize, no?"

"You are my prize, yes," he said. He spread his arms and moved forward to sweep her up in them.

"You're a beauty, you are, girl," he said. "A rare treasure."

"More rare than you know," she replied, pressing herself against him. Her breath was hot on his neck as her mouth found his flesh. He twisted his hands in her hair and drew her head back roughly, bringing his lips to hers. Something about the taste of her mouth raised a warning deep within him, but he ignored it, caught up in the passion of the moment, the thrill of the capture. Her hands ran up and down his body as she held him near, and she brought her mouth once again to his neck. This time, he felt a sudden piercing pain as she nibbled, then bit down hard, sinking impossibly long teeth into his flesh. He let out a scream and tried to break free, but she held him easily until he lost consciousness.

When he awoke again he was changed. He was immortal. Mara, the woman who had sired him, had walked the earth, she said, for three hundred years. She taught him the ways of the vampire, and over the next decades their love grew. He dropped the name Padraic and became known simply as MacKenna, and throughout the Southwest the legend of Mara and MacKenna was widespread. Parents used their names to scare their children into good behavior, and preachers turned to them to illustrate to their flocks the dangers of an impious life. Be like them, the clergymen warned, and you'll never see the inside of Heaven's gates.

Heaven, for MacKenna, was a different proposition altogether. He was living it right here on Earth, sleeping in the arms of the beautiful Mara by day and hunting with her at night. He had abandoned his old gang and his old way of life. When they needed money, he took it, either over a card table or from victims no longer in a position to complain. They stayed on the move, riding the rails or the Wells Fargo stage line from one frontier town to another, always staying ahead of those who would put an end to their way of un-life.

Until the day in 1901 when MacKenna's existence was changed once again. He and Mara had been separated, one of the first occasions in years that it had happened, while he collected on a gambling debt and she went ahead to Las Cruces to find them appropriate quarters. But while she was there, the local padre caught up with her. Armed with crucifixes and stakes and backed by a dozen men, they cornered her on a dark street and put a final end to her undead life. When MacKenna showed up on the next day's train, the story was still being told in fevered whispers all over town.

MacKenna flew into a rage, killing the priest and as many of the other men as he could find before riding out of town on a stolen horse. When he stopped running again, in the mountain town of Durango, Colorado, he was a broken man. He lived there for a harsh winter, on the streets, feeding when he had to and tempting the fates to destroy him as they had his lady love.

When they didn't—when he not only survived, but began to thrive in spite of the cruel conditions and his own self-destructive urges, MacKenna had an epiphany. Since he hadn't died, he thought, there must be a reason that he lived—a purpose larger than himself. Having achieved that small insight, he set about trying to find what that purpose could possibly be. He spent the early years of the century traveling. He spoke with every seer and shaman he could find, visited with spiritualists in London and Paris and New York, spent six months at a remote lamasery in Tibet and another six in the dark, shadowed forests of Eastern Europe meeting with witches and the elders of the vampire world. MacKenna traveled to Peru and up the Amazon, into the heart of Africa, and around the world to the Far East, China and Japan and Australia, in search of wisdom and special knowledge. The world raced on around him, one world war followed by another, economies booming and busting, the map redrawn again and again. He ignored it all, focused on unraveling the threads of information that he had found.

And bit by bit, piece by piece, he put together his plan, applying knowledge from a dozen different traditions of magickal thought. He moved back to the dry, dusty Southwest that Mara had taught him to love, eventually settling in Los Angeles because he could find the things he needed there, and he set about consolidating his power among the local vampire underworld.

Through it all, he had worked tirelessly toward this night. Since the spring of 1902, he realized, he had been driven toward this one specific goal.

"MacKenna," someone said. He snapped out of his reverie and looked up to see that DiNardo and Kravitch had brought in two young people, most likely clients of the club with which he shared a building. They were both dazed-looking—the vampires had probably drained some blood to quiet them down and make them agreeable. That was fine. He didn't want to hold a conversation with them; they only needed to be alive. MacKenna pointed at two altars in the center of the room, raised wooden platforms with grooves running around the outer rim to direct the blood, and piping that would ultimately drip the blood into the dozens of goblets MacKenna's acolytes had carefully placed there. Leather straps riveted to the table would hold the victims down.

"Put them there," he said.

DiNardo and Kravitch complied. The male sacrifice began to struggle, as he realized in spite of his haze what he was in for. But the vamps were too strong for him and managed to get both humans strapped onto the tables.

MacKenna looked around the room. Candles

were lit and positioned appropriately. Braziers smoked, releasing fragrant smoke into the air. The sacrificial victims strained against their bonds, where the last moments of their life energies would be put to good use. He rubbed his hands together, satisfied that his long journey toward destiny was nearing its final goal.

2

Glen Murphy's house was in a quiet, determinedly middle-class residential neighborhood in Culver City, where the streets were wide and the houses had grassy yards with old, tall trees that shaded them from the sun. At night, the upper reaches of the trees were barely visible in the reflected glow of the streetlights, their branches blocking only the silvery cast of the moon. No one was on the sidewalks, and only a few houses showed lights inside or out. In contrast to the rest of the city, this neighborhood truly was a bedroom community where everyone seemed to go to bed at the same time. The passing thought occurred to Angel that somewhere else in the city, far from here, people were working through the night to guarantee that the electric clocks and refrigerators and home heating-and-cooling systems of these slumbering masses continued to function, even during these hours of darkness. That might not seem as important as fighting evil, but Angel felt a kinship with those nocturnal workers who helped others sleep easier. *Most people don't wake up in the morning and thank the ones who didn't sleep,* Angel thought, pulling his GTX over in front of Murphy's house. *But maybe they should, once in a while.*

He rang Murphy's doorbell, hearing its tones from inside the house, loud in the still night air. *I'd feel bad about waking Murphy up if I thought he was sleeping,* Angel thought. But he had a bad feeling that if the delivery driver slept, it was the kind of sleep from which there would be no easy waking. When there was no response, he knocked on the door. This time, he thought he heard something—a human voice, but muffled. He knocked again, pressing his ear to the door. He heard the same indistinct sound.

Grabbing the doorknob, Angel twisted until he felt the lock snap. No inside bolts held the door, only the lock in the knob, which Angel knew could have been locked from the inside by someone leaving. With the door open, he could more clearly hear the voice inside. Murphy was gagged, no doubt, but calling for help.

"Can I come in?" Angel called, knowing that, unless expressly invited inside, no vampire could cross the threshold of a human's residence while that human lived—gagged or not.

The voice responded something that must have

been affirmative, for Angel was able to step inside. He followed the muffled cries to a bedroom closet and opened it. A pale-skinned, chubby man dressed only in striped boxer shorts and black socks was tied up tightly with ropes. With rags stuffed into his mouth and tied there with another strand of rope, he lay on the closet floor. A goose egg purpled the skin above his right eye. The smell of sweat rolled off his body in waves. He'd been here a while. Angel reached down and tugged the gag off him.

"Are you okay?" he asked the man. "Are you Glen Murphy?"

"What are you, crazy?" the guy responded. His voice was hoarse, but his indignation genuine. "Someone calls for help, and you ask if it's okay to come in?"

"I'm polite," Angel said. "You're Murphy?"

"Yes, I'm Glen Murphy," he replied impatiently. "Can you maybe untie me please?"

Only if you promise to put some clothes on as soon as I do, Angel thought. *And a shower wouldn't hurt.* But he chose not to say those things out loud, and instead bent to the task of freeing Murphy from his bonds.

"What happened to you?" Angel asked. "Do you know who did this?"

Murphy stood unsteadily, rubbing his arms and legs as to restore circulation to them. "Someone cold-cocked me when I came home last night," he said. "I never got a look at him." Mercifully, he reached for a pair of pants in the closet.

"Did you know that someone forged your signature and stole your UPX truck from the service lot?"

Murphy looked at Angel in surprise. "No," he said. "I mean, I was in the closet. But now that you say that, I might have an idea who did this."

"Who?"

Murphy fastened his pants and pulled on a shirt. "I was in a bar the other night, Benno's, on Sixth, and there was this guy in there. We got to talking, and he started buying me drinks and asking me all about UPX. How the trucks drive and how UPX works. I guess I told him the truck was going in the shop, and he even asked how it got checked in or out. He seemed like a cool guy, and I gave him my number, told him to come over some time. He must have followed me home and clocked me when I came in last night. Which reminds me—who the hell are you, and how do you know about my truck?"

There was no place in the small bedroom to sit except on the bed, and Murphy was there, pulling on his shoes. So Angel stood, somewhat uncomfortably in the cramped space. The floor of the bedroom was messy, with dirty clothes and car magazines scattered everywhere. "My name's Angel," he said. "I'm an investigator, looking into some crimes that were committed using your truck."

"L.A.P.D.?" Murphy asked.

"Private."

"Okay. I think I heard cops here earlier, but I guess they couldn't hear me calling for them, and they didn't try to break in like you did."

"They thought you checked the truck out yourself, so there was no reason for them to suspect you were trapped inside," Angel explained. "They were looking for you, but probably figured this would be the last place you'd hide."

Murphy shrugged. "Makes sense, I guess. Except for the part about thinking I took my own truck."

"The forgery was a pretty good one," Angel said. "Who was this guy from the bar? Did you get his name? A description?"

"I remember his name," Murphy said. "Not a name you hear much anymore. Homer, he said it was. Said his dad was a real baseball fan, back in the glory days. Didn't tell me a last name, though. He was just an average looking guy, I guess, pale skin, dark hair, regular features. About my height, maybe a little taller, six foot maybe."

The description isn't much help, Angel thought. *It could be the guy I saw in the deliveryman's uniform, with the truck. But it could also be about twenty percent of the population of Los Angeles.* "And he didn't give you a phone number, an address, anything like that?"

Murphy shook his head. "He was just a guy I talked to in a bar. Maybe if he was a lady I talked to in a bar I'd have gone for the phone number. You might have noticed from the state of my house, I'm a bachelor. But a guy—this guy in particular—I mean, with all these questions, I was just happy to get out of there at the end of the night," Murphy said. "He turned out to be kind of annoying, to be perfectly honest. After a while, I was sorry I'd invited him to come over."

"I know how that is," Angel said.

"I'll bet you do," Murphy replied. "Seeing as, with all the questions you've been asking, you kind of remind me of him. You sure you ain't brothers or something?"

Actually, we are in a way, being vampires, Angel thought. But he kept his mouth shut and shook his head. Murphy rose from the bed and led Angel back to the front door, examining at the broken lock.

"Looks like you did a number on this," he said.

"I was trying to save you," Angel pointed out.

"I know, I don't mean to give you a hard time. Just going to have to replace it is all." He stared at Angel for a long moment, then took a light jacket off a coatrack near the door and tugged it on. "Any more questions?"

"No," Angel said. "No, I guess not. If you think of anything else or hear from this guy Homer again, let me know." He handed Murphy one of his cards, which the man immediately pocketed. Murphy showed Angel out the door and followed him out.

Angel watched him head for his garage. Then the man stopped and looked at Angel again.

"What?" Murphy asked.

"It's just . . . you're going out? You know it's like two-thirty in the morning."

"And I've spent the last twenty-six hours on the floor of my closet, where there wasn't a lot to do but sleep," Murphy said. "Anyway, I've got to get that door fixed. I'm going to the twenty-four-hour hardware store."

"There's a twenty-four-hour hardware store?" Angel asked.

Murphy shrugged again. "It's L.A.," he said. "If you look hard enough, you can find anything."

3

Jarod Bennett looked barely older than Gunn, but he was the city-beat reporter for the *Herald*. A mug of coffee with cartoon characters on it steamed by his elbow, dwarfed on his crowded desk by reams of paper, a computer monitor and keyboard, a telephone, a stack of reference books and a copy of the massive Los Angeles telephone directory. Jarod wore a blue oxford shirt, corduroy pants, and a patterned tie loosened at the neck, with his collar button open. His sleeves were pushed up to his elbows.

ANGEL

Gunn suspected he'd learned how to dress like a reporter from the movies.

"It's a new-guy thing," Jarod said. He spoke with a soft but pronounced Texas drawl. "New guy puts in three overnight shifts a week until enough other new guys come along to bump him out of the rotation. I've been the new guy for two years now. Next new hire, I get moved to days."

"Bet you're lookin' forward to that," Gunn said. He sat in a visitor's chair next to the desk. The visitor's chair was really the desk chair from the empty work space next door, temporarily moved over. "Must be hard to work some days and some nights." *Although come to think of it, that's what we all do at Angel Investigations,* he thought. *Days, nights, and whatever's in between. Guess you just stop missing sleep when you don't get any.*

"Yeah, it's tough," Jarod agreed. "You never quite adjust. Your body is always out of whack, and it's hard to stay awake through a whole shift here, even when things are happening. You run on caffeine and pray for an adrenaline rush to get you through from four to six. Then you get home and you're exhausted from being up those hours, but you're also buzzed from the coffee. But you didn't come here to talk about my insane work schedule, as fascinating as I am. Shirley said you might know something about the poison attacks that have hit the city tonight. We're working up a big article about them

132

for tomorrow, but I have to admit, we're still kind of in the dark."

"I'm not sure how much help I'd be," Gunn said. "I know they're happening—"

Jarod cut him off. "Before you go on, is this on the record? Can I quote you on this?"

Gunn shook his head and held out both his hands in a warding-off gesture. "No, absolutely not," he said. "Way off the record. So far off you can't even see the record from here."

"All right," Jarod said. "Then why are you here? What's your interest?"

Gunn had known this question would pop up sooner or later and he'd prepared his response. "I'm an investigator," he said. "Private, not police. A client has been victimized by the attacks, and the family wants to find out what's going on. Specifically, I'm interested in how widespread it is."

"So you want me to help you, but you don't have any info for me?"

"I'll give you whatever I can," Gunn said. "But I don't know how much help that'll be."

Jarod took a drink from his coffee mug. On it, Scooby and the gang ran from a ghost, but the ghost had human legs, wearing shoes sticking out from under its sheet. He noticed Gunn looking at the picture. "I love that show," Jarod said. "All those crazy monsters chasing those kids around."

"I know the feeling," Gunn said.

Jarod put the mug back down. "All right," he said. "As far as we've been able to determine, the attacks have been concentrated in Los Angeles County, with just a few down in Orange County and one or two in Ventura and Riverside. They've focused on astronomers, astrophysicists, cosmologists, and the like—people who, if they weren't comatose, would more than likely be looking at the stars all night."

"They have?" Gunn asked, surprised.

"Your client doesn't fit that category?" Jarod asked.

"Uhh . . . well, he looks at the stars sometimes, but no. Not exactly."

"You've got to give me something," Jarod said. "Anything."

"Well, my information was that the targets were mostly people a little less mainstream. Magicians, astrologers, that kind of thing. I hadn't heard about any scientists."

Jarod smiled. "Now *that's* interesting," he said, apparently mulling this tidbit over in his mind. "That's a new twist. What do ya suppose the connection is between those kind of folks and space scientists?"

"I have no idea," Gunn said. "No clue whatsoever."

"Let's think about it, then. Rassle with it a little," Jarod said. "Astrologers, they definitely pay attention to the stars, right? So there might be a link there."

"Could be," Gunn admitted. But there was also the vampire angle he wasn't going to go into with this guy. *Angel isn't a target because he's a star watcher,* he thought.

"Now by 'magicians,' do ya mean stage magicians? Like David Copperfield and Lance Burton? Or something else? Which is what I'm guessing."

"Definitely in the something else category."

"So if I read between the lines a little, I'm guessing your client has something to do with the occult. And the other victims, the ones you know about, are also connected with the occult in some way."

"That'd be good line-reading," Gunn agreed.

"That makes sense," Jarod said. "There have been a couple of reports that didn't seem to tie together. A magick-shop owner on Melrose was found earlier tonight, for instance. One or two others. But for the most part, it's probably safe to assume that the occultists you're talking about tend to avoid publicity. If their family or friends found them unconscious, they might be a bit hesitant to call the cops or the press, am I right?"

Gunn nodded. The guy caught on fast.

"And magick, ritual magick, I mean, that often has something to do with the stars and planets, right? 'When the moon is in the seventh house,' and all that?"

"Not my area of expertise," Gunn said. "Seems right, though."

"So that just strengthens the story," Jarod went on. "We're definitely looking at some kind of organized plan. People all over the Southland, with whatever tenuous connection to the stars, are targeted by some kind of poison gas or whatever and put into comas, possibly all by UPX packages. The million-dollar question is, why? What's anyone got to gain from this? It's not a random crime, that's for sure. Too well plotted and organized."

"No," Gunn agreed. "I'm sure it's not random. But I'm not too sure about anything else."

"Yeah, well, that's where we're in the same boat," Jarod said. "I have more of a story than I did before you came in, but there's still a big chunk of it I'm missing. You find out anything else, you'll let me know?"

"If I can," Gunn said. He shook Jarod's hand and rose to leave. *Story'll never see print,* he thought. *None of the really weird stuff that goes down in this city ever does. It'll be killed before morning. If Jarod fights for it he'll be out of a job, but if he rolls over maybe he'll get off the night shift sooner than he thinks.*

Just the way this city works.

4

"Dear friend of Wesley's," Cordelia typed. Then she highlighted the line and hit DELETE. *Too casual,* she thought. *This should be serious from the start.* "To whom it may concern." She deleted again. *Too distant.* She decided to put off the salutation for now and work on the body of the message.

"Wesley Wyndam-Pryce and an unknown number of other—" *Other what?* she wondered. *Other British ex-Watchers who now run detective agencies founded by vampires?* She deleted "other" and went on. "Wesley Wyndam-Pryce and an unknown number of people associated with the occult in and around Los Angeles have fallen victim to—" She stopped typing again. *Does "fallen victim" sound too passive?* she thought. *Like, oops, I've fallen victim and I can't get up?* She deleted the phrase. " . . . have been attacked by an unknown assailant, who has rendered them comatose with some kind of altered Calynthia powder hybrid." *That's good,* she thought. *Hybrid. I just don't get a chance to use that word often enough.*

"As far as we can tell, everyone in the Los Angeles area who might be in a position to know the cure or antidote has been affected by these attacks. So I'm writing to you, Wesley's friends in other parts of the world, to see if there's anything you can do to help.

If you have—" *What?* she thought. *Experience? Knowledge? A clue? We could certainly use someone with a clue.*

Then the word came to her and she continued typing. " . . . expertise in sleeping spells, Calynthia powder, or any relevant areas of magick, please get in touch with me as soon as possible. Yours truly, Cordelia Chase." *That's dorky,* she thought, and deleted "Yours truly." She wrote "Sincerely" in its place and sat back to look at the whole message.

"Wesley Wyndam-Pryce and an unknown number of people associated with the occult in and around Los Angeles have been attacked by an unknown assailant, who has rendered them comatose with some kind of altered Calynthia powder hybrid. As far as we can tell, everyone in the Los Angeles area who might be in a position to know the cure or antidote has been affected by these attacks. So I'm writing to you, Wesley's friends in other parts of the world, to see if there's anything you can do to help. If you have expertise in sleeping spells, Calynthia powder, or any relevant areas of magick, please get in touch with me as soon as possible. Sincerely, Cordelia Chase."

That'll do, she thought. No salutation was really necessary. She added "Angel Investigations" after her name, to make it look that much more official. And she'd be sending the message on Wesley's own E-mail account to names in his online personal address book, so anyone receiving it would know that it was legit. She read over it once more, looking for anything stupid that she might have missed the first time. Finding nothing, she hit SEND.

Then she sat back to wait. Wesley had been restless for the last hour or so, squirming and moaning softly in his sleep. He kept breathing regularly, though, so she figured he was okay, except for the part where he wouldn't wake up. She hoped that his dreams were at least pleasant ones. *But from the look on his face,* she thought once, watching it contort in what looked like terror or agony, *I wouldn't put a lot of money down on that part.*

As far as she was concerned, E-mail was every bit as magickal as Calynthia powder and the rest of the ookiness she'd experienced at Angel's side. She knew there was a scientific basis to it, but not what that basis might be, any more than she understood the real reasons magick worked. Her assumption was that E-mail made its way around the world automatically, and that there weren't thousands, or millions, of people whose job it was to shuffle E-mails from point A to point B or point Z or both. But really, that was just a guess. Surely, she thought, there had to be people operating the various servers and switching points that were no doubt required for something as massive as the Internet to function. She remembered hearing somewhere that when there had been only a single phone company in the

U.S., and before automation had become common, the phone company had done a study showing that there would come a time at which it would have to employ every single adult woman in the country to work as telephone operators. No mention of men taking on some of the jobs or what they'd have done if some of the women hadn't cared to become operators. Fortunately, automation had intervened and kept them from having to deal with that probability. But Cordy had found the story fascinating just the same.

As she sat and wondered about that, the computer chimed to alert her to an incoming E-mail. She opened it immediately.

"Cordelia," it said. "I am Franklin Ayers Bishop, an acquaintance of Wesley's from New Zealand. My expertise is primarily aboriginal magick, which is what I came here to study many years ago, but I have more than a passing familiarity with other schools as well, including many sleep magicks. If there's anything at all I can do to help, please let me know."

This sounds promising, Cordy thought. *That is, if I can figure out the right questions to ask. If only he was a little closer—like, next door.*

She pressed her palms together and tried to think of how she should reply.

5

Angel used his cell phone to call the Host while driving through the quiet streets from Glen Murphy's place to Benno's. He was going to check out the bar at which the UPX deliveryman had met the guy he believed had attacked him. Caritas, the Host's karaoke bar, would be closed at this hour, but the green-skinned demon always stayed awake after closing to do his bookkeeping and straighten up, and his living quarters were in the same building, so Angel expected that he'd answer.

Unless he's on the victim roster, Angel thought. They'd checked in with him earlier, and he'd been fine. But Angel knew the Calynthia delivery crew was still out and about. Caritas was a demon sanctuary—in which demons of every stripe could congregate without fear—which would probably have kept him out of harm's way, but now that the bar was closed, he could be in danger. After a few rings, he picked up.

"Not Caritas," he said, sounding unhappy to be answering the phone at this hour, "because Caritas has gone to bed, and why the hell haven't you?"

"It's Angel."

"Question answered," the Host said, his voice a little more cheerful. "What's up, besides you, you nocturnal nugget of vampirehood?"

"Have you had any UPX deliveries tonight?" Angel asked. "Any packages you haven't opened yet? Any UPX drivers been around to see you?"

"Nobody has sent me anything," the Host replied. "And the only uniforms I've seen were two Waigan females dressed as leather nuns. The whole effect was very Village People, if you know what I mean."

"Did you see anything else strange tonight? Anything at all out of the ordinary?"

The Host paused for a moment before answering. "Does demonic spontaneous combustion count? Because there was this one incident. . . ."

"What happened?" Angel demanded.

"A Voktal. I don't know if you know them, genderless demons, all about parthenogenesis, but with a great voice for the old torch songs, you know? He/she was singing 'Hey, Big Spender,' and apparently got a little too heated up, because all of a sudden, *whoosh!* A big ball of fire. Scorched the stage, and even though I cleared the place early, I was up cleaning bits of fried Voktal off the floor and walls for more than an hour. No bacon for me for a while, I'll tell you. And if you're coming this way, bring some room freshener."

"Okay," Angel said. *That's strange, but doesn't sound associated with whatever else is going on,* he thought. "If anyone comes to the door tonight, don't open it."

"Deal. And I won't answer the phone, either, okay?"

"I think the phone's okay, but—"

"Hello! Joking, since you so rudely awakened me with one. Anyway, I know what you're going on about."

"Am I going on?" Angel asked.

"For you, oh laconic one, yes. You're worried about whatever got Wesley getting me too, right?"

"Yeah," Angel said. "It seems to be going around."

"Well, I just want you to know how much I appreciate your concern."

"Have you heard anything about it there?"

"Not really," the Host said. "There were whispers about it, but no one really wanted to talk. Business was off tonight, a little, and the word was that some of my regulars were a little under the weather. Hopefully not six feet under. You're okay, though?"

"I'm okay," Angel replied. He balanced the phone between his shoulder and ear, so he could make a series of hard right turns with both hands on the wheel.

"And the stalwart one? He's sleeping peacefully?"

"Like a baby."

"Anything I can do?" the Host asked. "Chicken soup?"

"And do what, pour it on him?" Angel asked. "He's not really so good with the eating and swallowing right now. But of course, if you could come up with an antidote . . ."

"Doing actual magick? Not my thing," the Host said. "But I'll make a few calls before I return to my much-needed beauty sleep, see if I can come up with anything."

"That'd be great. And be careful. They're still out there."

"Not for long, now that you're on the case," the Host said. "I'll give you a call if I get any results."

Angel pressed END and put the phone away. He had reached his destination, a bar deep in L.A.'s business district. This neighborhood was very busy during the day, and the opposite of busy at night. The neighboring high-rises were full of offices, mostly financial. By day, the buildings were full, the streets crowded. At this time of night, though, only skeleton staffs worked, if that: a few janitors cleaning offices, stock and commodities brokers keeping tabs on markets around the world. Lights showed in office windows in staggered patterns, but the buildings were mostly dark. The retail businesses at street level were geared toward the day crowd too— delicatessens, travel agencies, electronics stores, and the like, all long since closed for the night, most with metal gratings pulled down over their display windows and doors.

At Benno's the neon was turned off and the door was locked, but the metal grate that would be secured over the front had not been lowered yet. So someone was inside. Angel pounded on the glass.

After a few minutes, he saw someone shuffle out from a back room, looking weary and more than a little perturbed. The man flipped a white dish towel over his shoulder as he came. This was Benno, presumably.

When the guy reached the door, he peered out at Angel. "We're closed!" he shouted indignantly.

"I know," Angel replied. "I'm not here to drink." He pressed his business card against the glass. "I just have a couple of questions for you. It's very important."

Benno shrugged and unlocked the door. "It better be," he said. He was a short, round man, wearing gray pants and a gray cardigan sweater over a white shirt. He had a damp apron wrapped around his waist, and the dish towel flung over his shoulder indicated that Angel had interrupted him washing the night's glasses. Thin hair had been combed all the way across his head in a failed attempt to cover a bald spot. A bushy mustache, as gray as his clothes, covered his upper lip, and equally bushy eyebrows floated over his tired eyes.

"I'm sorry to bother you," Angel began, "but it's literally a matter of life and death. Do you know your customers well?"

"Some yes, some not so much," Benno answered. He sounded a little nervous to Angel, who put it down to having a stranger pound on his door after the bar was closed. That probably happened on a fairly regular basis, but more than likely opening the door to said stranger was a far less common occurrence.

"Do you know a guy named Glen Murphy? He's a UPX deliveryman. Maybe he even comes in uniform sometimes."

Benno smiled, which was indicated primarily by a twitching of his mustache, as if it had come alive and was trying to wriggle off his face. "Sure, I know Murphy. Good customer. Always pays his tab, never looks for credit. Doesn't bend my ear too much. I like those features in a man."

"He was here a couple of nights ago."

"He's here most nights."

"A couple of nights ago," Angel said again. "And he was talking to a guy. This guy was asking him a lot of questions, mostly about his job. It was probably a pretty intense conversation. You remember that?"

Benno scratched his chest for a moment. "Nope," he said. "I mind my own business, unless I'm invited into a conversation. If Murphy was talking to someone, they kept it between themselves. Sorry."

"This guy might have been in his early thirties, dark hair that covered his ears, a long forehead, small eyes. Remember anybody like that?"

"That's pretty vague," Benno said.

"I know. This guy looks like a lot of people."

"Wish I could help you. Be a lot more interesting than the dishes waiting in the back. But if there's nothing else . . ."

"I guess not," Angel said. He pressed his card into Benno's hand. "If you remember who Murphy was talking to or see the guy again, call me. My cell phone's on all the time."

"Gotcha," Benno said. "I'll do that."

Angel thanked him and returned to his car. *Another dead end,* he thought. The night was full of dead ends, seemingly as many as there were stars in the sky. And meanwhile, Wesley's life was at stake.

No time to sit and worry about it, he knew. He had to keep moving. Until he had an answer, a way to wake Wesley, he had to stay on the go.

6

The darkness was total, infinite. Wesley literally couldn't tell if his eyes were open or shut, except by feel. Generally, he knew, even in the darkest of places, there was some light. Moon and stars shone on benighted fields and filtered through the leaves and branches of the deepest forest. The glow from streetlights crept around or between curtains to cast faint illumination into a sleeping chamber. In a dark room the human eye would adjust, the pupil widening to let in as much light as was available, Wesley knew, and within fifteen minutes a person would be able to see as well in the dark as most animals. But in here, with his lantern snuffed, there was nothing, no trace illumination for the eye to latch onto. He knew his senses still worked— he could hear groans of shifting earth and the patter of falling rubble, could smell the coal dust choking the air, could feel the heat generated by the millions of tons of compressed coal surrounding him, but he might as well have been struck blind, for all that he could see.

Mustn't panic, he told himself. Panic would only disorient him more, send him running, perhaps, in the wrong direction, or cause him to bash his head in on a beam or jagged point of rock, finishing the job the cave-in hadn't managed to complete.

He still knew, he was sure, which direction led to the main shaft. He didn't know precisely where the cave-in had occurred—it could be ten feet away or a hundred or farther. With no lantern the blackness was all-consuming, but that didn't mean he had been cut off from the rest of the world, he realized, just that he couldn't see anyone else's lanterns from this position. *So the thing to do,* he thought, *is to follow the tunnel back toward the main shaft. That'll be where I'll find anyone else who might still be down here. If I come across a barricade, then I can deal with it at the time.*

Carrying the useless lantern in his left hand, in case he reached a point where he'd be able to safely relight it, he extended his other hand until he could feel the slightly oily tunnel wall. If he kept the wall within reach, all he had to do was keep walking, and he would eventually come across the point where Rollie and the Welshman, Dafydd, had been having their lunch. Rollie had been working much nearer the main shaft, so if he could find the man he'd be almost back to safety.

He'd been walking for just a few minutes when he heard mumbled voices ahead. His heart leaped; he had to fight the urge to run toward them, reminding himself that a headlong dash in such pitch darkness was the most dangerous thing he could do. He did pick up his pace just a little, still keeping his fingers touching the wall, and he called out. "Hello! Hello, Rollie?"

A moment later his call was answered. "That you, California?"

"Yes!" he shouted, his relief a palpable thing. "I mean, it's Wesley, yes! My lantern's out but I'm heading your way!"

"Easy then, lad," Rollie called back. "Take it slow, we're goin' nowhere!"

Wesley didn't like the sound of that, but he forced himself to take careful, measured steps, head ducked, fingers scraping along the wall. Finally he saw light, a faint glimmer reflecting off the wall ahead, and then he rounded a corner and was almost blinded by the glow of four lanterns all held out toward him. He blinked against the sudden, relative brilliance. Part of him wanted to weep, seeing these men and their light.

But then he remembered what Rollie had said. *Going nowhere.*

"Are we . . . trapped?" he asked.

Rollie stood there with Dafydd and two other miners Wesley didn't recognize. Two of the men held their lanterns in the other direction, away from Wesley, to reveal a pile of broken wooden beams and giant chunks of rock clogging the tunnel.

"Aye," Dafydd said. "'Twas Tommyknockers after all."

"What do we do? Surely we can dig through it."

"We've just been debatin' that," Rollie said. He gestured to one of the other men, who carried a caged canary in one hand. "The bird's alive, so we've air t'breathe. For now."

In the glow of the four lanterns, Wesley got a better look at Rollie than he had earlier. The man had always seemed familiar, but in the dark, Wesley had been unable to place him, believing that he'd simply seen him on the way in or knew him from day to day work in the mines. But now, looking at Rollie, Wesley realized that his own proper place was not in the mines; he worked in Los Angeles, with Angel and Cordelia and Gunn. He didn't know how he'd gotten here, but it wasn't a place he belonged. He'd been transported through time and space, or he was suffering an agonizing dream, or something, but he knew who he was and where he belonged and this was not it.

But at the same time he understood why Rollie looked so familiar to him. In his grandparents' home there had been an old, framed photograph, one of a group of family photos arranged on the mantel of the fireplace. This particular photo, a primitive picture in black and white, faded and cracked with time, had been of several men in miner's black, coal dust smudging their skin and haunted looks in their eyes. One of the men, he'd been told, was his mother's grandfather, who had worked his whole life in the mines. Wesley had never known his great-grandfather, but as a boy he had looked at the photo thousands of times, wondering what the old man's life had been like.

And the man in the photograph, the one in the center who had been pointed out as young Wesley's great-grandfather, had looked just like Rollie. Heavy brow, thick mustache, jagged scar extending from eye to lip—the man who called himself Rollie was the very image of the one in the photo, as if he had stepped out of the frame and come to life. Wesley glanced around at the other miners, to see if they looked familiar, but he had never really paid much attention to the other men in the picture, focusing instead on his own ancestor.

There was something more, Wesley knew, if only he could put his finger on it. The reason he'd looked so long and hard at that particular family heirloom. There had been a story that went with the picture, he was sure.

If only he could remember what it was . . .

Three O'Clock

1

"I did exactly what you told me," Benno insisted. Homer thought the bartender sounded scared. *Of course*, he thought, *if I was a human and I was looking at two full-on vamps, I might be a little scared too.* "I told him Murphy was a regular, because any number of people could've confirmed that. And I told him I couldn't remember you, Homer, and couldn't identify you. Just like you said to."

"That's good, Benno," Homer said. Speaking clearly with the fangs out was still a little awkward, even though he'd been a vampire for many years now. But he had been told that he'd get used to it in time. And time, for a vampire, was a limitless proposition. Especially after MacKenna's plan paid off. Then there would not only be time, but freedom. He'd never have to wear the human face that he grew to hate more and more with each passing day. "Do you know where he went after that?"

"No," Benno replied. "He didn't say. Just took off. I have no idea where to."

"But he left you a way to get in touch with him." It wasn't a question.

"He gave me a business card. It's got a cell phone number on it."

"Then you should call him up," Lenny said. "Tell him you need to see him again."

"You think he'll buy that?" Benno asked.

"You just got to sell it," Lenny said. "That's the ticket. If you can sell, he'll buy."

"I don't know. . . ."

Lenny moved close to Benno, putting his face right in front of the diminutive barkeep's, letting the man see the length of his fangs and the glare in his eyes. Benno glanced over at Homer, who simply nodded. "There's no room for argument here, Benno. You'll do it. You know we're the wrong guys to fool around with."

"Y-yeah," Benno said. "I'll do it. Sure. Just let me get the ph-phone."

"Take a couple of deep breaths," Homer suggested. "You don't want to sound all nervous and stuff when you talk to him."

"D-deep breaths," Benno repeated. His hands shook as he tried to snag the phone off the hook, and the receiver slipped from his hands, clattering to the floor. He swore under his breath and picked it up again, fumbling with it as he brought it to his ear. Lenny took Angel's card from his quivering fingers and dialed the number. Homer could hear it start to ring.

He paced as the frightened man waited to talk to Angel. Homer had followed Murphy around for a couple of weeks on MacKenna's instructions, and had—*well, "enlisted" might be the word,* he thought—Benno in his quest to get close to Murphy after he'd seen the UPX driver entering the bar in uniform on a fairly regular basis. He started coming by occasionally himself, letting Murphy see him so that when he finally approached the man he was already a familiar face. And he slipped Benno a few bucks to greet him like an old friend whenever Murphy was around, heightening the appearance of a regular patron who could be trusted. Then tonight, when Angel slipped through the cracks in their plan, the possibility had occurred to Homer that the vampire detective might be clever enough to track down Murphy, who would certainly point Angel in Benno's direction. So he'd warned Benno that Angel would be around and given him strict instructions on what to say. Changing to vamp-face and crushing part of the solid wooden bar with his

154

bare hands had been enough to persuade Benno to do as he was told.

And Benno had complied. But now they needed more from him, and the man was being a little less forthcoming. According to MacKenna, Lenny was supposed to be running the show now—*running his mouth is more like it,* Homer thought, *and that's what got him in trouble with MacKenna in the first place.* But Homer was the brains of the team and they both knew it. So Homer paced and thought while Lenny muscled the bartender into compliance. Regardless of MacKenna's orders, that was the way they had always worked together, and so far it had been a successful team-up.

Apparently Benno's call was answered, so Homer listened to his end of the conversation.

"Hello, Angel? This is Benno," the barkeep said. "At the bar. I saw you earlier tonight, asking questions about Murphy. That's right. Well, I remembered something that might help. Yeah, in my receipts, a credit card slip. You should really come over and take a look. No . . . no, you really gotta see it. Yeah. I'll be here."

Then Lenny hung up the receiver and smiled at Benno. "See how easy that was?" he asked.

"Yeah," Benno replied, still terrified. Before, he'd believed that Homer and Lenny were criminals, but they'd been willing to pay him off and that had been good enough. When Angel came into the picture, though, Benno had become frightened, and they'd had to show their true faces to scare him into submission. And that meant, Homer knew, that they couldn't just walk away from the guy now.

"Are you okay, Benno?" he asked. "I mean, are we okay?" He gestured to Benno and then back at himself and Lenny. "Because I think we've grown close, over this experience, don't you?"

Benno looked a little taken aback. "Yeah, sure. Sure we have. I'm o-okay, you know? If you guys are."

Homer came closer to the man. "I was worried there, for a few minutes, Benno. Thinking that maybe you didn't like us as much as we like you. That's not true, though, is it?"

"No. No, I like you fine. Both of you."

"That's great," Homer said, stepping still closer. "Gimme a hug, Benno. I think we need a big, healing hug to put this all behind us."

Benno didn't look at all sold on that idea, but he didn't have any room to maneuver. Homer put his arms out and wrapped them around the stout man, and Benno's arms came reluctantly around Homer, hands resting ever so gingerly against his back.

Homer squeezed tighter and sank his fangs into Benno's neck. His mouth filled with blood, rich and delicious, more so because of the fear-born adrenaline coursing through the bartender's veins. He drank deep.

When he was done, he released Benno, and the lifeless body crumpled to the floor. "That was good, Benno," he said. "A good hug. I needed that."

2

MacKenna stood in the exact center of the circle that had been painted on the floor and closed his eyes tightly. He held his arms out to his sides, palms up as if to catch falling snowflakes. At this moment, while he was certainly the focus of attention in this room, he was also the center of the universe to all vampires around the world, whether they knew it or not.

Most did not. Most of them would only find out what he was up to after the fact. Secrecy was vital. He had let some of the vampires of Los Angeles know approximately what his plan was, the ones who had already sworn their allegiance to him, because he needed their protection and assistance. But that was as far as he'd gone. Once he was successful, then the whole world would know. And he would be revered as a savior. No—he would be worshipped.

He felt the power build in him as he stood there, in the appointed spot at the appointed hour. Palms up, he spoke the prescribed words, in a language that was not his native tongue, not even native to his species. *"Ia Nagog ithnai gtthonic clevander,"* he intoned. *"Ditherin Luodium vernustul chreee."* He repeated the odd phrases three times, louder each time. On the second time, he felt his fingertips start to tingle, as if static electricity buzzed around him. The third time, all the hairs on his body stood on end.

Then he spoke the words a fourth time, at a full-throated shout, and felt the power course through him—the power of the dreamers, all their restless energies flowing through the city and into his body. The dreamers were like an enormous battery, feeding him power through the mystical tendrils created by bits of his own essence mixed in with his particular Calynthia recipe, tendrils that reached far and wide across the slumbering Southland. As they slept, their pent-up energies released into him, fueling him for the task ahead. And a huge task it was, demanding all the strength that he could bring to it.

What MacKenna sought to bring about was nothing less than a vampiric homeland here on Earth. For too long had his kind been driven into the shadows, kept from walking the streets at will as the hated humans did. Vampires were more powerful than humans, but humans had one ally that gave them power, that kept the legitimate rulers of the planet at bay.

That ally was the sun. Soon, that ally would be defanged. Vampires would no longer have to fear the sun, and then their true potential could be unleashed. Untethered, vampires would rule all, and mere humans would cower before them.

The problem, MacKenna had decided early in his un-life, was the globe's constant spinning, bringing the glorious night, but all too soon restoring the despised sun to the heavens. The rotation of the Earth, though, was not something that could be stopped, not without risking the elimination of every life form from the planet, including vampires, and rendering it a cold, lifeless ball floating in space. No, that wasn't where the answer lay.

But in discarding that possibility, MacKenna had hit upon another one. More research had shown this other possibility to be plausible, a genuine chance to build a vampire nation here on Earth. The planet's rotation, he had learned, couldn't be stopped—but the tilt of the Earth on its axis could be changed. Was, in fact, already being changed, through the works of man. Vast reservoirs, artificial bodies of water created in the northern nations of Russia and Canada, primarily, holding trillions of tons of water within them, were subtly shifting the axis. The North Pole, true magnetic north, had drifted twenty-seven inches toward Hawaii in the past fifty years. Slow progress, but progress nonetheless.

So MacKenna decided he would speed the process up. Through the use of the magick he had studied for so long, he would tilt the Earth, changing its axis suddenly and dramatically so that his chosen area would never again face the sun. Global climate would be affected, though he didn't know precisely how. Murderous storms, earthquakes, tidal waves, and other natural disasters would no doubt ensue. But vampires had little to fear from such dangers; they would only reduce the total numbers of the human population, making vampire-rule that much more of a likelihood.

When MacKenna was finished the Earth, like the moon, would have a permanent night side and day side. One side would be hammered by the sun; the other would be protected from its killing rays. On the night side, vampires would reign supreme. And on the day side, humans, left without their natural ally, would be raised as cattle, meat for the taking.

It would all happen tonight.

MacKenna had impressed himself with his own brilliance. He needed more power than he possessed himself, so he envisioned a way to draw power from dozens of other powerful individuals, draining them of it as they slept. At the same time, he chose as power sources those people who would be most likely, were they awake, to notice the Earth straining to slip its axis and to raise an alarm. Not only witches and wizards, occultists and astrologers would fuel his magick, but astronomers and cosmologists, anyone who might be watching the stars by night and realize when they began to shift in the sky. Certainly, there would be amateurs, out with their telescopes, who might notice something—but anyone they'd call to confirm their data or sound a warning would already be asleep. And those beginners wouldn't have the power to prevent his ritual from succeeding. Anyone who noticed in other parts of the world would have to sit by and watch it happen—none of them could get to Los Angeles in time to halt the inevitable.

MacKenna had thought of everything. Once he'd shifted the planet on its axis, the correct alignment of moon, stars, and sun to restore it wouldn't come around for another several hundred years. By which time it would be far too late. Humans would have no memory of ever being anything but slaves. And vampires, whose memories were longer, would be happily getting used to the new order of things. The proper order.

The way things always should have been would become the way things were. Vampires would take their rightful place at the top of the world's pecking order. And MacKenna would take his own seat at the top of the top.

He felt the power course through him, and he smiled.

3

Angel tucked the phone back into his pocket. Benno had sounded terrified, but that was probably to be expected if he had really come across a key to finding Glenn Murphy's attacker. He made a quick series of right turns that sent him back toward Sixth and the vacant streets of the financial district.

Two blocks from the bar, he spotted a UPX truck parked just beyond a street lamp's cone of light. He figured Benno could hang on for a couple of minutes longer while he checked it out. *Seems like a strange place for a UPX truck,* he thought, *which should, this time of night, be parked in a lot somewhere awaiting the next day's packages.* He drove around the block and slowed when he reached the truck again, this time from the rear. Sure enough, the number emblazoned on its door was RD-1472, the number of the truck he'd run across earlier.

Angel chuckled softly to himself. *Pretty lame,* he thought. *Setting a trap for me at Benno's and not hiding the truck any better than that.* He continued through the intersection and around the block again, making his way to the alley that ran behind the bar. He left the car at the mouth of the alley and found the rear entrance, a stained and dirty door that Benno probably only used to dump his night's trash in the Dumpster outside. Angel looked through the grease-blurred window and held his ear close to the door to listen. No sounds came from inside.

He turned the doorknob as quietly as he could, feeling the lock break under his grip, and pulled on the door. It was held by a deadbolt about head-high. That one would be harder to snap, at least without making some noise, but there was nothing he could do about that. He gave the door a sharp tug and the bolt tore free of the jamb, splintering wood as it came. Angel braced himself, expecting a Calynthia missile to come sailing at him, but it didn't. He sniffed the air inside the bar; fresh blood mingled with the smells of stale liquor and shattered hopes.

Still no attack. Angel went inside, senses alert for any danger. With each step he anticipated an attack that didn't happen. Finally, in front of the bar, he found Benno's corpse, torn at the neck by sharp fangs, white from loss of blood. A fine spray of blood coated the side of the bar, but the bulk of it had fed Benno's attackers. In spite of himself, the scent aroused Angel's ancient hunger, and he turned away from the body.

The bar's front door was unlocked, so that was the escape route the vamps had taken. Maybe they hadn't meant to lay a trap at all, Angel realized. Maybe they had simply stopped to tie off a loose end after dumping the stolen truck. If that was the case then Angel was fresh out of clues, unless they'd conveniently left a map or an address inside the truck. With Wesley's life at stake, he had to check, had to try whatever he could to track them down.

Almost reluctantly, he left the bar by the alley door through which he'd entered. Barely had the door shut behind him when a flash of motion caught his attention. A glint of light in the darkness outlined the projectile that flew at him with a bullet's force. Angel threw himself down as the tube shattered against the side of the building, Calynthia potion splashing in a semicircle around its point of impact. Angel rolled, dodging the spatter. He regained his feet as the second one flew at him. Again he dodged, yanking the bar's back door open and diving inside. As he slammed it, still another projectile slammed against its outer surface. Angel dashed into the main barroom.

The second vampire, the one who'd been driving the truck earlier, waited at the front door, a crossbow in his hand loaded with a wooden bolt. He took careful aim at Angel's heart and squeezed the trigger.

Angel ducked and the bolt sailed over his head. As he pushed himself up and toward his attacker, the vamp reloaded and loosed another bolt. Angel sidestepped it, but it drove deep into his calf, and the searing pain forced him to the ground under a table. He reached up and tipped the table, overturning it just in time to stop the next bolt. Gritting his teeth against the burn, Angel gripped the bolt's end and tugged it from his flesh and muscle. He would heal, but it would definitely slow him down for a while, he knew—just when he could least afford to be slowed.

And in the meantime he was surrounded. He heard the bar's back door swing shut, which meant the first vamp, the one with the Calynthia-shooting weapon, was making his way into the bar behind Angel while the one with the crossbow and seemingly infinite number of wooden bolts waited in front of him.

This really stinks, Angel thought. *I should be able to take out two vampires with my hands tied behind my back. Or a bum leg.* But in the narrow space of the bar, with one in front and one behind, he would be exposed if he left the relatively safe position he had fallen into, bar behind him and table in front. And if he didn't leave it, they could just work their way to the sides and pin him there. *Which means,* he thought, *that if I'm going to do anything at all it's got to be now, before they can take their positions.*

"Give it up, Angel," the vampire in front of him snarled. "This can still go down the easy way if you let it."

Angel took a guess that the "easy way" would involve him going to sleep painlessly, like Wesley. Or maybe ending his life in a puff of vampire dust. "I don't think so," he replied. "But it can go easy on you if you throw down your weapons and surrender."

The vampire chuckled, an unpleasant throaty sound. "Yeah, right," he said. "You're the one who's trapped."

Already figured that out, Angel thought. He decided to gamble that the one behind him was less likely to shoot him than the one in front. After all, he'd have to make sure that his comrade wasn't hit with the Calynthia, unless they had some sort of vaccine against its effects, so he'd have to be careful about where he shot it. In any case, Angel reasoned, if he could take out the crossbow guy then he would also have a distance weapon he could use against the other. With a grunt of pain he stood and lifted the table, holding it in front of him as a shield and a ram, and charged through the bar, plowing over tables and chairs. The vampire with the crossbow let out a surprised cry and Angel heard him scrambling for the door. But Angel drove the table forward and felt the impact as he barreled into the vamp. He kept advancing, and then they were at the front window, the vampire screaming now as he crashed through the glass, being cut in a dozen places. Angel gave a last heave and the vampire fell out onto the street in front of the bar. Then he spun, still gripping the table's legs, just in time to use it to bat away the oncoming Calynthia bomb.

In the bar's dim light he recognized the vamp with the gun as the one he'd fought earlier, on the truck. He needed to take this guy out before one of those Calynthia projectiles found home—even a few drops of the stuff, he guessed, could knock him out, and he couldn't risk that. So he snapped a leg off the table he held and dove out through the window. The vampire on the sidewalk had pushed himself up to a sitting position, but as Angel came through the broken window he held the shattered wood of the table's leg out before him like a spear. It sank into the vampire's chest and he exploded in the typical cloud of dust. His crossbow clattered to the sidewalk, already loaded with another wooden bolt. Angel scooped up the weapon and whirled around, aiming and pulling the trigger as he turned. A Calynthia projectile was already in flight toward him and the still-uniformed vamp was reloading, but the bolt sailed true and plunged into his heart. As he flattened himself on the sidewalk, Angel heard, rather than saw, the vampire burst into dust and his weapon fall to the floor. The Calynthia bomb sailed out into the street and exploded harmlessly on the pavement.

Angel limped back into the bar and looked at the fallen weapon. Its load of Calynthia had exploded around it, so he didn't dare pick it up. Hearing distant sirens closing in, he went back out through the alley door and hurried to his waiting convertible. Since he'd dusted both his assailants, he was back to having no leads. He'd see what the UPX truck offered—it was far enough away, he thought, to escape the notice of cops hurrying to see the bar. The discovery of Benno's drained body would keep them at the scene for a while anyway. But the way the rest of his night was going, he didn't anticipate that the truck would yield much in the way of clues.

On the way, he pulled out his cell phone and dialed Gunn. The phone was answered almost instantly. "Yeah?"

"Gunn," Angel said. "Anything?"

"Nothing," Gunn replied, sounding disheartened. "I found out who the targets are, and where. But it's nothing that helps us."

"Who and where?" Angel asked.

"Besides the ones we already knew about," Gunn told him, "astronomers, rocket scientists—anyone who works or studies space seems to have been targeted. All over L.A. and the immediate surrounding counties."

"Space?" Angel echoed.

"Yeah. The stars, the sky, you know. Anyone might be lookin' at the stars ain't lookin' there tonight. You come up with anything?"

"Not really," Angel said. "I found those vampires I told you about earlier, the two with the stolen UPX truck. Or they found me. But unfortunately they didn't survive to answer any questions. We know this thing is much bigger than just them, though. I want you to round up your guys and meet me. We'll shake down any vamps we can find until we figure out what they're up to. Someone's got to know something."

"Wouldn't be hard for someone to know more'n we do, that's for sure," Gunn said, "seeing as we know just about nothing. Where do you want to meet?"

"Your guys keep track of vampire activity in the city, right?"

"That's what they're all about," Gunn said. "'Course, they like to take 'em out soon as they find 'em. But they might know of a nest or two."

"Find out," Angel said. "And let me know. We've got to move fast."

4

"Thanks for your response, Mr. Bishop," Cordelia had written after receiving the E-mail from New Zealand. "Here's my deal. I am not actually Ms. Wizard or anything. If you have any ideas for spells or anything I could do to help Wesley, I'd love to hear them, but I might need you to walk me through it. We don't know precisely what put him to sleep, but it was a green spray that was inside a booby-trapped box. When he opened it, it blasted him and he fell right to sleep. Angel thinks it was a Calynthia powder mixed with something else or enchanted in some way, but he doesn't have the details. Is there anything I can do?"

While she waited for a response, Angel called. He was on his cell phone and reception wasn't great, but she could make out his voice.

"Cordelia," he said. "How's Wesley?"

"Not much change," she said. "Still the Posturepedic poster boy. He's been thrashing around a little bit, moaning. For a minute I thought he was having a really good dream, if you know what I mean, but now it sounds more like a nightmare. And you know, this time of night, I'd almost change places with him in a second. It's really hard to stay awake when there's no one to talk to except a guy who's sleeping."

"Just keep a close eye on him."

"I am, Angel. I don't know what I'd do if anything happened, but I'm watching him like an eagle. Or is it a hawk? I guess one watches like a hawk, but with an eagle eye. Something like that, anyway."

"Good. How are you coming on research?"

"Could be better," Cordy replied. "I got an E-mail from some magician-type Wes knows in New Zealand, who thinks he might have some ideas. But unless he can do long-distance spell-casting, I'm not sure what good it'll do."

"Anything's worth a try," Angel said. "In the meantime, we know that there are vampires involved in whatever it is that's going on. So you might want to take, you know, precautions."

Vampires, Cordy could deal with. In fact, she was a lot more used to them than she was to mysterious green fogs putting her friends into comas. After Angel hung up she went to the weapons cabinet and removed an assortment of crosses, with which she surrounded the bed on which Wesley tossed and turned—one at each compass point, just in case Wes really was the target and someone came back to finish the job. Then she took out several stakes, which she placed around the room for easy access, and a crossbow with a handful of wooden bolts, which she put on the desk next to her computer. *Any vamp trying to get into this hotel tonight will encounter some serious resistance,* she thought.

While she prepared her arsenal, the computer chimed again. Another E-mail. She looked at the monitor and saw that it was from Franklin Ayers Bishop. She opened the E-mail and read through it quickly.

"Cordelia," it read. "From what you have described, I believe I might know what's been done to the Calynthia. As you know, I believe, it typically exists in a powder form, usually a white, talc-like powder. But to create the kind of booby-trap you described, the perpetrator would need a more explosive mixture, something that would fill the air around the box. That's best accomplished by changing the Calynthia to a liquid form which would then be injected into a pressurized container. Break the seal, the pressure forces the liquid Calynthia from the container, and presto! A sleep bomb. The green coloration disturbs me a little, as more typically liquefied Calynthia is more of a tan color, like coffee with cream in it. So my supposition is that something more was done to the Calynthia, to give it some other property that we have not yet puzzled out. If you can answer some additional questions, I will try to have a solution to you post haste."

If I had any more answers, Cordelia thought, stifling a yawn, *I'd have given them to you in the first place.* But she couldn't argue with a guy who was thousands of miles away, especially since he was only trying to help. And so far, he was the only one of Wesley's so-called friends who had even bothered to respond. So she bit her tongue and read through his questions. The list was long and many of the questions were incredibly detailed: queries about the specific mechanism of delivery, the exact timing of the various attacks, the nature of the attackers, the consistency of the Calynthia compound used, the odor of it, and any particular sounds that may have accompanied its delivery.

Most of the questions she had no answers for, and in her reply she said as much. She did pass on Angel's information that vampires were involved, and she told Bishop what she could remember about the specifics of the attack. The box had been taken away, though, and the mess carefully cleaned up, so there were questions that she couldn't answer without opening the hermetically sealed trash bag and examining it again, and she didn't dare do that. She couldn't open herself up to the possibility of falling under the Calynthia's influence, which would not benefit Wesley at all. So she wrote what she could and sent the E-mail shooting across the world's digital network, back to New Zealand.

5

"We must try to find a way out," Wesley urged the other miners. "We can't just sit here."

"They'll be lookin' for us, lad," a miner named Davies argued. He was the one holding the canary's cage, and he looked to Wesley like a rugby player, with broad shoulders and arms knotty with muscle and sinew, a thick neck that looked as stout as a tree trunk. His nose had been broken multiple times, and Wesley guessed he was a fighter in the outside world. He remembered having heard that boxing and other matches were popular sport among the miners. He wasn't sure why—he figured that if he had such a dangerous job, he'd probably want a soothing hobby, perhaps flower gardening, to while away the after-work hours. It probably had to do with machismo, he thought. Mining was a real man's job.

"A cave-in big as the one we been through," Davies went on, "they'll 'ave felt all the way in town. There's plenty of folk about, and the search parties're already workin' their way down. If we move about, chances are they'll come 'ere in search of us and pass us right by."

"I would agree with you," Wesley said passionately, "if we had any idea how big the cave-in was or how many tons of rubble are between us and the main shaft. But we don't, and we don't have any idea if we have enough air to hold out until they manage to break through to us."

Randall, the other miner Wesley hadn't met before, a diminutive man barely five feet tall— *Man?* Wesley thought. *Barely more than a boy, surely not yet out of his teens*—pointed to the cage that Davies still held. Rags that must once have been white were tied around Randall's knees, for no reason that Wesley could discern.

"'E's still got th'bird," Randall pointed out. He tried to sound confident but it didn't work; emotion cracked his voice and fear inhabited his eyes like a ghost in a house of death. "So we know we've got good air yet."

"Yes, for now," Wesley said. "But for how long? That's the question. Once the bird dies, how long do we have? An hour? A day?"

"Hours at best," Rollie replied. His voice was low and soft, as if held down by the weight of the rock pressing down over their heads. "Just hours."

Wesley gestured back the way he'd come. "And back there, anywhere along this shaft, are there other side shafts? Any other ways to get back than through the part that's caved in?"

"Aye," Dafydd said after a moment's hesitation. He stroked his stubbled chin with filthy black fingers, leaving long streaks on his beard. "Aye, there're one or two played-out shafts. They've been closed now for some time."

"Closed, but at one time they met up with the main shaft? Or some other way out?"

"'Tis possible they did," Dafydd said. "Possible. Could be they were only ever got to through this tunnel, but I don't know that for certain."

"One thing is certain, though," Wesley said. "If we stay in here and help doesn't come in time, we're dead men. And I don't know about you, but I'd rather take steps to save myself, if they're available, than to depend on others to save me."

"Then ye're not only a fool," Davies said, "but a damn fool. Ye'll waste yer own breath fightin' against the mine when there might be fifty blokes on the other side workin' to save yer skin."

"Believe me," Wesley shot back. "I've been in tight spots before, plenty of them. And I've had my life saved by others more times than I care to count. But if there's anything I can do to improve the odds in my favor, I intend to do it. You can sit down and die if that's your pleasure, but I hope you'll work alongside me and help save us all."

The photo on his grandparents' mantel came back to him then, the miners with their red-rimmed eyes-though he'd never known before that they were red, only that their eyes were strange looking somehow-blinking against the unfamiliar sunlight. They all looked gaunt and frightened, Wesley remembered, and though the relief was evident on their faces, they weren't smiling, as one might expect of people who'd just been saved from certain doom. They looked too exhausted to smile.

What Wesley believed the photo showed was men who had saved themselves, who had fought for their freedom from the Earth's deadly embrace. They were glad to be out in the light and the air but they were grateful to no one save themselves for their rescue. Had they been looking upon their saviors, Wesley was sure, their expressions would be different—joyous or relieved, not the serious and composed faces they wore.

No, he was sure they had saved themselves, and he was sure that the photo showed this particular group of men. Rollie, he had become convinced—and it made no sense, except that he was dreaming and in dreams anything could be true—was his own great-grandfather, and the photo he'd looked at so often as a boy was of the day his great-grandfather came out of the earth after a massive cave-in. He could almost hear his grandfather telling the story now, describing the way everyone had assumed the men were dead and how the church was being read-ied for the funerals, the women weeping and the miners who had made it out speaking in hushed, re-spectful tones of their lost brethren. No one had ex-pected to see them again, but they had appeared anyway, and the photo had been taken just as they emerged from what should have, by all rights, been their mutual grave.

There was more to the story, details he couldn't bring to mind. He couldn't remember, for instance, how they had been rescued. *That would be a great help,* he realized. *If only I could recall what had happened, I'd know what we should do.* But it wouldn't come, no matter how hard he tried to dredge it up. The memory could have been lost in a mental cave-in, he realized, hidden behind some obstruction he couldn't find a way around or through.

"I'm wi' Wesley," Rollie announced suddenly. "I say we choose one of the old routes. Mayhap it's closed off, but it might be an hour's diggin' to get through instead of a day's."

"I'd expect it from one as green as 'im, Rollie," Davies said scornfully. "Don't believe I've ever seen 'im down the pit before, in fact. But I thought ye'd 'ave known better. Ye'll just waste air by tryin' t'dig. Ye'll doom us all."

"Seems we're doomed anyway," Rollie said. "I'd as soon give it a go and die makin' the effort as sittin' on me duff doin' naught."

"I tell ye, they're already searchin' for us," Davies countered. "What d'ye mean, doomed?"

But Randall had figured out Rollie's meaning and stood, mouth working but no sound coming out, pointing at the cage in Davies's grip. Wesley followed the young man's finger.

The canary lay on the cage floor, lifeless.

"What d'ye think now, Davies?" Rollie asked him. "Are you still so certain we've any time left to stand here arguin'?"

"Reckon not," Dafydd put in. "If we're goin' t'dig, let's get to diggin', shall we?"

Rollie picked up his pick from where it leaned against the shaft's wall, and the other men followed suit. Rollie went first, shouldering his way past Wesley and heading back into the depths of the tunnel. "This way," he said quietly as he passed. "There's an old shaft, played out long ago, down here. If we can get into it, we ought t'be able to find our way into another pit that's closed ten years or more, now. But naught's ever really closed, down here—they're all just holes in th'ground, and where there's a hole, there's hope."

"Thank you," Wesley said. "For agreeing with me, I mean."

"No call t'thank me," Rollie replied. "You were right. Davies was the one bein' a fool. Simple as that."

"Yes, well, it sounds simple when you put it that way, but life often doesn't work out so easily."

"You look a wee bit young to know so much about life, boy. And green as a spring twig, like Davies said. But there's somethin' about you just the same. Somehow I can't help trustin' you."

Wesley smiled, knowing the other man couldn't see it as they made their way through the tunnel by the light of a single lantern. "You know, I feel the same way about you."

6

Stanley Liebersoll strained against the bonds that held him. His strength was returning now—the people who had attacked him had drained enough blood to make him compliant but not so much that he was rendered unconscious for more than a few minutes. So he'd been awake and frustratingly, agonizingly unable to respond, as he and Jackie were brought into this basement chamber, carried to broad tables, and strapped down, facing the cavernous roof of the deep space.

His neck burned. If he didn't know better—if he didn't know they were mythical creatures—he'd have sworn he was attacked by vampires. Their faces had looked strange, distorted, their teeth impossibly long and sharp, but that must have been a trick of the light, he thought. His abductors had gone for the neck because it was a convenient place to find veins that carried blood back and forth to the brain, so draining it from there would make him and Jackie light-headed and unable to resist. They hadn't really used their teeth, he convinced himself, but some weapon, some surgical instrument maybe, that would draw out a lot of blood in a short time.

He was able to turn his head a few centimeters, just enough to see that Jackie was bound to a table much like his. She seemed unconsciousness still. Either that or she was paralyzed from shock or fear. She stared straight up, through eyes that might have been blind, for all the expression they exhibited to Stanley. Her profile was every bit as fine as he remembered it, the curve of her nose and the sculpting of her lips and the line of her jaw each perfect elements fitting together in a perfect whole.

He hoped the worst was past, that they'd have to lay here for a while during whatever ritual these strangers were performing—he recognized now that that's what it was, some bizarre rite like out of one of the horror novels he read—and then would be released unharmed when it was all over. He didn't believe in real magick, but knew that there were plenty of people who did, and even some who deluded themselves that it really worked. But Stanley was convinced that no demon would be summoned tonight, no powerful forces would marshal here to declare war on the surface world, so there would be no need for the human sacrifice that he had convinced himself that he and Jackie were meant to symbolize.

Even so, he hoped it wouldn't take too long. The table was uncomfortable. It didn't feel perfectly flat, but instead had points that jabbed up into his back and legs at various intervals. He couldn't quite figure out what the purpose of such an unpleasant table was, and when he found himself trying to, he purposely stopped himself. Instead he sent his thoughts back over to Jackie, the willing beauty he'd met tonight, because the thought that was there, on the other side of the line he didn't want to cross, was just too horrible to allow himself to contemplate.

Four O'Clock

1

The dark gray stone building had been a cheap motel, a skid-row fleabag, in the days when the long, low building next to it had been a bus station. But consolidation in the interstate bus business had shut down the station, and the hotel, deprived of its steady stream of customers arriving from points east with no plans, family, or friends and not much money, had closed soon after. Both buildings had stood empty ever since. Officially empty, that was—in reality, the former hotel had become a haven for the undead. A vampire nest.

Gunn and his crew had raced from point to point throughout the big city for the last thirty minutes.

They tried to keep tabs on vampire activities around Los Angeles, but as he'd told Angel, his friends didn't tend to be as interested in surveillance as in total destruction. Sometimes they watched a nest for a night or two, trying to figure out how many vamps were in it, what kind of attack they'd need to make, what time of day the nest was at its most vulnerable. But they kept their observation as brief as possible, knowing that as long as they were only watching, people were dying. Vampires needed to feed constantly, so any night they let the vamps survive was another night some human would fall victim to their wretched hunger.

So mostly what they did when encountering a nest was to move in, during daylight hours if possible, to catch the bloodsuckers sleeping and dust them. When they had to go in at night, they did so—more cautiously and always in teams. The end result was the same, though: no more vampires.

Tonight they'd checked out two rumored nests and two locations they had already placed under surveillance. An empty building that had once been a free-standing bank, a ranch house in Baldwin Hills, an apartment upstairs over a tattoo parlor, and finally this abandoned hotel. Vampire activity had been observed in each of these places over the last few days, and they had all been considered targets for missions tonight—until the Calynthia attacks had changed everybody's plans. But tonight the bank, the ranch house, and the apartment had been vacant, as if all the vamps in town were busy someplace else. *No way they'd have been thoughtful enough to just move out,* Gunn thought, *so there has to be some other explanation. What bothers me is the idea that the explanation ties into the magick dust that's going around.*

But at the old hotel next to the shuttered bus station, vampires had been spotted moving in and out. The watchers sat inside a broken-down van parked a block away, looking through smoked windows with army-surplus night-vision equipment. They saw movement inside on all four floors of the hotel, as well as individual vamps darting out, presumably to feed, and then back in again.

Satisfied that this target would do, Gunn called Angel and settled down to wait. What was it that Jarod Bennett had said? Something about praying for an adrenaline rush to carry him from four to six in the morning. Gunn understood that. He felt anxious about what was coming up and determined to help Wesley if he could, but even so the lateness of the hour was wearing him down. He could use an adrenaline rush right about now. He spread his weaponry out around him to inspect it all before the action started.

The van shifted as someone came toward him, and he looked up. "I'm all itchy," Rio said, settling down next to where Gunn sat on the musty-smelling carpeting of the van's floor. Gunn had brought a variety of stakes in different lengths and his hubcap axe. He'd thought about making some wooden knives, like that guy Blade used in the comics, but decided it really wasn't worth the trouble. Stakes worked just as well, and if he lost one it wasn't a big deal. If he lost a knife he'd spent hours working on, he would feel a whole lot worse about it. "Can't wait to dust some o' them bloodsuckers," Rio went on. "Why don't we just go in and get it over with?"

"We're waitin' for Angel," Gunn replied. Rio already knew this, but apparently needed reminding.

"So we're gonna let a vampire lead us into a vamp nest? What's wrong with this picture?"

"Ain't nothing wrong with it," Gunn said, "except the way you're lookin' at it. Angel's a right guy. I already told you the vamps are up to somethin' big tonight, and we got to know what it is. We go in there and dust all these vamps, we're gonna lose any hope of findin' out. We need a little patience, and then we'll go in and we'll show some restraint."

"What you mean, restraint?" Rio asked him.

"I mean we need some prisoners who can talk to us. We can't just kill 'em all right off the bat."

"You ever taken vamp prisoners?" Rio wanted to know. "I mean, that don't sound too easy."

Gunn chuckled softly. "Since when has anything worth doing ever been easy?"

"Well, he better hurry, is all I got to say. Longer we sit here, better the chances are that they'll sniff us out. Then things'll go different—we're sittin' ducks inside this van. Be like openin' a can o' sardines for them vamps to come and get us."

"Man's on his way," Gunn said. He picked at a fingernail with the point of a stake. Rio had a point there. They didn't even have the full crew here—the rest was waiting with the War Wagon half a mile away, so the vamps wouldn't see it and be tipped off. It would be here in minutes when he made the call—but if the vampires tumbled to this van, then they might not have minutes to spare. "Just give him a little while," he said, sounding more confident than he felt. "He'll get here and we'll go in."

2

As Gunn had instructed him to, Angel left his car a couple of blocks away and covered the last part on foot. They must have been watching; as soon as he approached the van Gunn had described, the rear door swung open and he was motioned inside. Half a dozen guys were in the van, Gunn included, making it crowded and hot.

"Where are they?" Angel asked.

Gunn cocked his head toward an abandoned

hotel across the street. Ironwork letters on the side of the building spelled out R YALT N RMS. "Royalton Arms," Gunn translated. "Former garden spot of skid row. Anybody with fifteen bucks and a strong stomach could get a room for the night. Roaches and rats included, no extra charge."

"How many are in there?"

"Don't know," Gunn replied. "Last night we counted thirteen or fourteen. Enough to put it onto tonight's target list. But so far tonight we've only spotted four. There's been movement inside but the windows are mostly boarded over so we can't tell for sure if we're just seein' the same ones again and again. We've only counted as definites the ones that have shown themselves outside."

"So we really have no clue how many are inside," Angel observed.

"Basically, right," Gunn said. "Seems to be emptier than last night, for sure. Which goes along with your theory that the vamps in town are up to something, and it's happenin' tonight, so they're not stickin' close to home."

"Do we have a plan?" Angel asked.

"Plan is we go inside and waste 'em," George offered.

"I told all you dogs, we need some prisoners," Gunn pointed out. "Don't dust 'em all. We need to keep at least two. Now, I don't want anyone goin' in alone—buddy up, teams of two or more at all times.

You go through a door solo, chances are you're not comin' back out."

There was a general murmur of assent; everybody knew the drill. Gunn got on his cell phone and called in the War Wagon. When it pulled up to the front the rest of them would charge inside. The Wagon would wait outside to take care of any vamps trying to escape.

A minute later Angel heard the roar of the truck's engine. "Here we go," Gunn said. They burst from the back of the van and ran toward the hotel as the War Wagon lumbered up the street from the other direction. Gunn had a stake in one fist and his axe in the other; the rest were equipped with stakes, crossbows, swords, axes, and the like. The War Wagon was heavily armed with a stake-shooting cannon, smaller wood-projectile shooting weapons, a battering ram front, and armored sides for the protection of those aboard it. Angel carried nothing, but under his sleeves he had a spring-loaded device that would instantly put a stake into each fist when he needed them. He passed the others and hit the front door first, bursting through it. Gunn came in right behind him.

The lobby was a small, seedy-looking place. Two chairs stood against a wall, looking like secondhand kitchen chairs rather than what one might expect to find in a hotel's waiting area. The counter stood by the opposite wall, surrounded by thick bulletproof

Plexiglas, with a small opening to pass money and keys through. Walls had been painted with layer after layer of graffiti. Trash had piled up over the years; the floor was awash in stray papers, bottles, cans, and other debris. Angel figured the bottles and cans were probably remnants of homeless people who had wandered in out of the dark only to become meals for those who lived upstairs.

There were no vampires in evidence now. Gunn gestured toward a narrow stairway that led up and away from the lobby. "Up there," he said. He and Angel went up shoulder to shoulder, taking the stairs three at a time, always alert for any threat from above. At the top of the stairs were six doors, all closed. Four of them still had numbers nailed to the wood.

Behind them, two more of the guys came to the landing and the rest continued up to the next floor. Gunn divided the hallway into halves: three doors on the right and three on the left. He pointed to the ones on the left. "Angel and I will take these," he whispered. "You guys take those."

Chain and Rondell nodded. Angel and Gunn went to the nearest door and Angel aimed a sharp kick just under its knob. The door splintered and flew open. There was no one in the room, but a flash of movement at the window drew Angel's attention. It was a vamp, diving to the street outside rather than confront those who were invading its nest.

From the street below, Angel heard the ratcheting sound of the War Wagon's weapons and a short, abruptly ending scream. *One down,* he thought.

They surveyed the rest of the room quickly, determined that it was empty, and moved on to the next. This time, Gunn kicked in the door. Two vamps waited inside, in full vampire face. They lunged at Gunn and Angel as they entered the room. Angel filled his fists with wood and met the first one in midair, driving his stake through its heart. It exploded in a dark cloud and Angel tumbled through it to the bare floor beyond. Spinning around, he saw Gunn swing his axe in an upward arc. The sharp edge caught the vamp in the throat and its head flew from his body. Beheaded, this vampire also burst into dust.

As he caught his breath, Gunn looked at Angel. "Thought we needed some live ones."

"We do," Angel said. "But not the first two. We'll keep the last two."

"Remember, we don't know how many's in here."

"I know," Angel said. "But there are still a few. I can smell them."

"Well, let's see what the next room smells like," Gunn said. They continued down the hall. From the room opposite they heard the sounds of battle and the death-cries of vampires. It sounded like things were going well.

3

Upstairs, things were not going so well. On the second floor, Rio and Cosmo had taken the rooms on the right side of the hallway, while Albert and George took the left. When they were done with this floor, they'd move up to the next one.

But when they went into the second room on the floor, things got ugly. The first room been empty. This one turned out to be full. Four vamps, three of whom were built like linebackers, were waiting just inside the door. Rio had played a little football in high school, back in Alamogordo, New Mexico, before his young wife Janice—or former wife, he supposed, since she had up and joined a whacko religious cult on him—had followed her newfound friends to L.A. He'd tracked her to the city, but far too late. The cult that Rio had thought was an off-kilter religious group was in fact a traveling band of vampires. They had made her one of their own.

He found them living in an abandoned movie theater, and had gone in armed only with a couple of stakes and a head full of rage. Inside, he had discovered that he was vastly outnumbered. As he prepared to die, Gunn and the guys came charging in— they'd been watching this very nest, getting ready to make their move, when Rio had come from nowhere and moved up the schedule a bit.

Inside, Janice had offered Rio the same treatment she'd received. Turning her down was the second hardest thing he'd ever had to do.

Driving a stake through her heart was the hardest.

But Gunn had held the other guys off while he did it, and encouraged Rio, telling him that he understood what he was going through. He'd been there himself, Gunn had said. Later, he'd told Rio the story of having to dust his own sister, and a powerful bond had been forged between them. After they'd polished off the nest, Gunn had invited him to join the group.

But now it looked like his brief membership might be at an end. Two of the bloodsuckers grabbed Cosmo. Cosmo screamed for only a moment, but then the largest of the vamps clamped a strong hand over his mouth, and lowered its own open mouth to Cosmo's throat.

Meanwhile the other two, including the smallest of the bunch, who was still bigger than Rio, had grabbed him. Rio plunged the stake he carried into one's chest but missed the heart, and the vamp flailed in pain, backhanding him across the face with claws that tore his skin. He fell back into the door-jamb and watched in horror as the vampire tugged the stake from its own chest, tossing it aside as if it was nothing more than a nuisance. Rio dug into his weapon belt and brought out another stake. But his back was pressed against the jamb, and all four

vamps now had directed their attention toward him.
If he squeezed out the door, he'd have to turn his
back to them. He was pretty sure that would be the
last thing he'd ever do. And it wouldn't help Cosmo
a bit.

The largest of the vamps lunged at him, eliminating any more time for strategizing. Just before the
creature plowed into him, a whistling sound
whisked past him and a wooden bolt sank into the
vamp's chest. The vampire just had enough time to
look down in surprise before he bloomed into a dust
cloud. Rio took advantage of the other bloodsuckers' momentary shock to leap at the smallest of
them. He caught the little one in a powerful
embrace, holding the vampire close and driving the
stake through its back, into its heart. His arms were
suddenly empty, vamp dust filling his nostrils and
blinding him for a half-second.

From the hallway, Albert and George came in,
Albert loosing another bolt from his crossbow into
the heart of one of the other vamps. George carried
a long-bladed broadsword, clutched in his fist as if
he were a knight of the Round Table. Rio had
laughed when he'd first seen George carrying the
weapon, but now George pressed into the room,
swinging the sword at shoulder height. The final
vamp threw Cosmo aside and tried to dodge, but
George was too fast for it and the sword's blade
sliced it cleanly through the neck. Its head flipped

over twice and then hit the floor, and the vamp burst into a dark cloud at the same time.

Rio bent over, hands on his knees, and blew out a long breath. "I owe you guys," he said. "Big time."

"Just lucky we didn't find any on our side of the building, I guess," George said.

"Hope we're not too late to help Cosmo," Albert said, eyeing their fallen comrade's body. "Let's get him out of here." George joined him, taking Cosmo's legs, and Albert lifted him by the shoulders. Blood trickled from his punctured neck, but he gave a soft moan as they lifted him.

4

Angel knew without being told the reason Gunn fought alongside him. He and Gunn had the most experience battling vampires; it would have made much more sense for them to split up, each with a less-seasoned partner. But with anyone other than Gunn at his back, Angel would have as much to worry about from his supposed ally as from the enemy. Gunn's crew didn't trust Angel, would never trust him, it seemed, even if they watched him kill a million vampires.

They had finished off their floor and then, with Rondell and Chain in tow, had dashed up the stairs

STRANGER TO THE SUN

to scour the next. There were only a couple of vamps left on that floor, though. Most of them had gone out the windows and run up against the waiting War Wagon, and the remaining ones fell easily under the brutal assault. Leaving Chain and Rondell to mop up, Angel and Gunn moved on to the top floor. It was getting to be time to take captives, and Angel trusted himself and Gunn for that job more than he did the others. In the heat of combat it might be too hard for the others to restrain themselves.

This floor seemed to be the main living quarters. The smell of blood was as thick as woodsmoke in a winter campground. Where most of the rooms on the lower floors were devoid of furnishings, the first one they entered here had two beds and some other furniture shoved into it and an assortment of personal items scattered around. Vamps didn't tend to go in for grooming aids or sentimental memorabilia, but a few of the ones living here had saved body parts from what must have been favorite victims—a skull sat on a dresser, a flap of skin from somebody's chest was nailed to the wall over a bed like a teen's concert poster, and a severed hand stood upright on the windowsill.

"Nasty," Gunn said.

"Yeah," Angel agreed. "Some vamps don't just kill; they more or less worship death. Looks like we've found that kind."

"Nasty," Gunn repeated.

"Come on," Angel said. "Next room."

"You sure we got to let some of these monsters live?" Gunn asked him. "Because I got to tell you, these vamps seem especially evil to me, and I wouldn't mind dustin' 'em all."

"We need the information," Angel reminded him. "We have to know what's going on tonight. Wesley's life might depend on it."

"Yeah, I know. Just checkin'," Gunn said. "I didn't save his tail from zombie cops just to throw it away again 'cause I'm disgusted by some vamps that are freaky even for the freaks."

Angel led the way out of the room and back into the hallway. He sniffed the air, working his way from door to door. Finally he stopped in front of the third door on the right. "They're in here," he said. "At least two. Let's take them alive."

"Too late."

"You know what I mean," Angel replied. He caught Gunn's eye. They both nodded agreement. Angel reared back and kicked the door in.

For a split second Angel thought he was facing Darla and Drusilla. There were two vamps in the room, both female, one with blonde hair and the other with long dark tresses. They stood against the far wall, hugging each other, fear on their human-looking faces. Trying to look like victims, maybe. He didn't buy it for a second.

But these weren't the two female vamps who had

meant so much in his life. "It's a trick," he warned Gunn. "Vampires don't get as scared as these two look. It's not in their nature."

"They are convincin', though," Gunn said. "Must be Academy Award season."

"Please," the blonde one said. "Don't hurt us."

"Okay," Angel replied. "It's a deal. You tell us what we need to know, we won't hurt you. How's that?"

"Anything," the brunette pleaded. "Just tell us what you want." It released its friend and stepped toward the two men, hands falling to its sides, slowly, as if drawing attention to its lissome, all too human-looking form. "You can have anything you want."

"I know," Gunn said. "'Cause we'll stake you if we don't."

The brunette took another step forward and lowered its head as if in shame. But then the head came back up again, vamped out, fanged mouth twisted in a horrific smile, and it lunged between the two of them, lashing out as it went.

Angel caught its wrist and spun the vamp around, using its own momentum to smash it face-first into a wall. The creature let out a yelp and tried to pull away. Instead of letting go, he twisted its arm up behind its back and brought his other one around its neck, yanking it toward him. The brunette struggled but couldn't break his grip.

Gunn and the blonde, meanwhile, faced each

other, Gunn armed with his menacing axe. The blonde hadn't vamped out, and looked every bit the frightened human it pretended to be, cowering against the wall at the intrusion of these two dangerous men. Angel knew that Gunn understood it was an act, though. He was at full alert, coiled like a spring, ready to slice it in two if it so much as moved.

"What—what do you want?" it asked.

"Information," Angel said. The brunette tried to pull herself from his grip but he just wrenched on its arm. It whimpered in pain and was still. "There's something big going on tonight. Most of the vampires in the city seem to be there. This nest isn't at capacity, so we're guessing that even some of your own are there. We want to know what and we want to know where. Whichever one of you starts talking first gets to survive. But only one."

"You can't be serious," the brunette said. It started to go on, but it was drowned out by the blonde's voice.

"They're in Downey," the blonde said, the words tumbling out like a waterfall. "A warehouse, off Rosecrans. It's behind a club."

Angel released the brunette just long enough to bring one of his spring-loaded stakes into his hand and drive it through its heart. He was already on the move toward the blonde as the brunette went up in dust. "Keep talking," he said menacingly.

"There's a rave club there, I know, and the vampires are meeting in an underground chamber behind it. I haven't been so I don't know all the precise details, but that's what I heard."

"It's a start," Angel said. "You can come with us until we know you're telling the truth." He took the blonde one by the arm and led it toward the door, pushing it through ahead of himself and Gunn.

It had barely cleared the door when there was a sudden movement from the other side—Rio, thrusting a stake at the vampire's chest. Angel tried to yank it out of the way, but Rio's attack was too far along by the time he saw it. The stake penetrated flesh, tore through muscle, shattered bone, and pierced the blonde's heart. Angel was left with a handful of dust, which he loosed and let pour onto the ground.

Angel turned on Rio, furious. "Why'd you do that?" he demanded. "I said we needed prisoners."

"Hey, I didn't know she was a prisoner, man," Rio said, defiance in his voice. "She come through the door all by herself. I thought she was gettin' away."

"I had her," Angel shot back.

"Well, I couldn't see that. Even if I could, look at you. You're a bloodsucker, same as she was. How's I supposed to know you wasn't helpin' her escape?"

"Because I said so," Angel retorted.

"And I did too, Rio," Gunn put in. "I told you, Angel's one of us. You trust me, you trust him."

Rio held his ground, looking at Gunn through

eyes narrowed with rage. "Maybe I don't trust you then."

"Maybe you need to take a hike," Gunn said. "You don't trust me, you don't belong in this crew. We got to cover each other's backs. Can't do that unless we trust each other."

The others were all gathered around—Angel noticed that a couple of them held the body of a fallen comrade, but even as he watched, the young man moaned and writhed in their arms. Everyone else who had come into the hotel with them was still alive—and everyone watched the tense confrontation with Rio. Angel knew he had to stay out of it. Now that Gunn had spoken up, if he interfered it would undercut Gunn's authority.

"You want me gone?" Rio asked. "Fine, then. I'm gone. Just don't come lookin' for me when you need a good man."

"I wouldn't," Gunn said. "Because a good man can follow orders and put the team ahead of himself." He looked at the rest of the crew. "Anyone else got a problem with that?"

The others looked back at him steadily, but no one answered. Rio pushed through them and went down the stairs. After they heard him exit the building, Gunn said, "Let's go." They all started down then, Gunn and Angel bringing up the rear.

"Bad scene," Gunn said quietly. "There's a lot of tension in the crew as it is, 'cause of all the time I been spendin' with you guys. Then to send someone away 'cause he didn't take your side . . . Let's just say it's gonna be a topic of conversation. Not the good kind."

"I stayed out of it because it's your team," Angel said. "But you know what? I don't really care what your internal politics are. I only care about one thing tonight, and that's saving Wesley. So let's get to Downey."

"Maybe we can figure out what that vamp chick meant," Gunn agreed. "But when we get there, we're just gonna get blasted by more of that Calynthia stuff, right?"

Angel nodded. "Most likely," he said. "You know what they say about crossing bridges."

"Yeah, I know what they say. But we're gonna get to this one pretty soon. Be a good thing if we had a plan."

5

After Stanley Liebersoll had been strapped to the table for what seemed to him like an interminable length of time, things started to happen. Jackie had begun to stir, finally, her gaze catching his, her eyes wide with the horror of the situation she found herself in. But as she tried to find her voice, two of their captors came to them and gagged them with foul-tasting rags. They held each other's eyes until another man approached them with a wicked, curved-bladed knife in his hands. Stanley was certain this was the end for them. He'd never see his family or friends again, or his school, or even the cruddy kitchen at A Santé. And from the tears that suddenly flooded Jackie's eyes, running the mascara that rimmed them, she must have felt the same way.

But it wasn't. As the leader's voice droned on in the background, this man carefully used his knife to cut away Stanley's shirt, right down the middle. He peeled the two sides away from Stanley's chest, then tugged the fabric from beneath Stanley so that he lay, half-naked, on the table. Then the man turned to Jackie and did the same. Now she looked away from Stanley, ashamed or embarrassed to be seen by him. He tried to look away but couldn't; her pale skin glowed in the candlelight like white marble or alabaster sculpted by a master's hand. *Beautiful,* he thought. *And I'll never touch her again. . . .*

A different person approached them, this one a woman with a cascade of blonde hair almost to her waist. She carried a goblet with a brush handle sticking out of it. Working on Jackie first, she dipped the brush into the goblet and drew out a gold-colored paint, with which she made strange but precise designs on the girl's exposed flesh. Jackie tried to squirm but the straps held her tight, and the woman was able to complete her task quickly. That finished, she came to Stanley and did the same to him. The paint was cold and unpleasant, almost grainy, as if there were sand or something mixed in with it. But he was tied down just as firmly as Jackie was and couldn't get away from the brush's touch. When the woman was done she moved away. Still, the man who seemed to be running things kept up his droning, indecipherable monologue.

Tearing his gaze away from Jackie, Stanley arched his back the half-inch or so that he could and twisted his neck, trying to see what else was going on in the vast chamber. He found the man he thought of as the leader, with his mouth speaking words that seemed never to have been meant for human voice, arms spread wide. A greenish glow surrounded the man, not from the candles but almost as if an aura or an energy field was coming from within him.

And before him, suspended in the air, was a globe made of pure light. Stanley thought he could even make out, limned by spidery traces of light against darker patches, the outlines of the continents: the Americas, then Australia and the vastness of Asia running into Europe, with Africa below, as the globe slowly turned. There was something not quite right about it, though, and it took him a moment to figure out what. Then it dawned on him. Because his own head was twisted and tilted at a bizarre angle, he hadn't been able to distinguish it right away, but he was used to seeing a globe with north at the top and south at the bottom and the continents more or less lined up between them. This one, on the other hand, was tilting as it revolved, so that North America, for instance, was almost at the Equator.

Suddenly the pitch of the man's voice changed, the tempo altered, and dozens of other voices joined with his. At the same moment, the woman who had painted him and Jackie reappeared in Stanley's field of view, only this time she didn't have the paint but the sharp-edged knife. Beside her was the man who had wielded the knife before. He came to Stanley's table and turned a wheel—it was just out of Stanley's range of view, but he could tell by the motions of the man's arms what he was doing. And he felt the sharp protrusions of the table's surface pressing up against his back, biting into his flesh now, being forced through his skin, and he finally realized what they were for.

The woman came closer and pressed the knife against his chest. He couldn't recoil away from the blade without jabbing himself on the many spikes burrowing into his back, and he couldn't escape the spikes without forcing himself up against the blade. The spikes below, already opening his skin, were no doubt already spilling his blood onto the table, where its furrows would direct it to vessels like the ones he could see under Jackie's table. He was reminded again that he'd initially thought these people were vampires, and now he supposed that he had been right. But he didn't think about it much longer because the pain and the cold overwhelmed his mind and his senses, and by the time the woman's blade sliced his chest open he could barely even feel the pain.

6

MacKenna's throat was getting dry, and the sound of fresh blood spilling from the tables' plumbing into the waiting cups was almost too much to bear. But he held his position, speaking the required phrases, doing his best to ignore the sound and the rich aroma of fresh blood emptying from the bodies of the sacrifices. The power with which the Dreamers imbued him enabled him to go on, to continue speaking, arms outspread, much longer than he ordinarily would have. That and the simple, visceral pleasure of watching the Earth tilt on its axis as he spoke carried him.

The vampires in the room, nearly a hundred strong now, filed past the tables, each one lifting a goblet and drinking from it, then putting it back in the exact same location to catch any more blood that might flow into it. They repeated this process three times and then returned to their places along the walls, their voices once again joining MacKenna's.

And the world turned, and the world tilted, and eternal night fell upon the land.

7

The flames in the lanterns the other miners carried burned blue now instead of yellow. Wesley, though he couldn't have said how he knew it, understood what that meant. The buildup of methane in the shaft they were trapped in was reaching dangerous levels. The lanterns kept the flame contained within a protective gauze screen that dissipated much of the heat while allowing only light to escape. When methane touched the flame, it burned more blue, but as long as the flame stayed behind the screen it wouldn't ignite the methane. If it escaped the screen, though—and that could happen through as simple an action as swinging the lantern too quickly, so that the air caught the flame and pulled it out through the gauze, or by trying to blow the lamp out with a puff of breath—the methane would explode. Also known to miners as firedamp, methane was released by the very act of cutting coal from the seams. Ordinarily, a complex system of baffles and wind generated by a furnace blew through the tunnels, keeping the methane concentrations at relatively safe levels. But no wind blew through this shaft now because the cave-in had sealed it off, and enough firedamp had leaked in from the seams they'd been working, or perhaps released by the cave-in itself, to kill the bird and blue the flames.

All in all, Wesley knew, the situation was dire indeed. If they even survived such an explosion, what would be left in the shaft would be afterdamp. Carbon monoxide. It'd kill them as surely as an explosion would. And if the methane concentration was high enough, it would only take a spark to set it off.

Wesley pointed at Rollie's lantern. "Firedamp," he said.

Rollie nodded. "Aye," he agreed. "Seen it. Lamps down, boys." He set the lantern on the floor, and motioned to the others to do the same. They did, and the flames went back to yellow, casting more light than the blue had. Methane was lighter than air, so it filled the upper part of the shaft first. For a moment Wesley was heartened by the comforting yellow glow of the lanterns, but then he realized that his head was still up in the thickest part of the methane, breathing as much of that as he was oxygen. And the methane was being replaced by the coal seams, while the oxygen wasn't. *We have to get out of here, and quickly,* he thought. *But the very act of striking a pick against stone might be enough to spark, and any spark might be the one.*

"What do you think?" he asked. "Do we dare dig?"

They stood before a brick-sealed opening into an old shaft. Old diggings were off-limits and were often bricked over to enforce that rule, as well as to block in any firedamp that had seeped into them. But on the other side of that brick wall was a shaft that might possibly lead to a larger shaft, and safety.

Rollie shrugged, though Wesley could hear the motion, the rustle of fabric, better than he could see it. "We daren't," he said. "Digging could kill us. But if we don't dig we're dead anyway, for certain. There's not near enough air down here t'keep us alive much longer. So weighin' probable death against certain, I say we dig and dig fast."

"I still think ye're makin' a mistake," Davies argued. He had abandoned the canary's cage at the cave-in site and just carried his lantern and pick now. "Ye'll kill us for sure."

"I think Rollie's right," Wesley said. "We must dig. We can't wait for someone to come get us."

"'Tis a pity we can't blast," Dafydd observed. The Welshman, Wesley had learned, was a fireman, one who set charges to blast away rock and expose the seams that the other miners would work. Blasting would certainly clear away the brick wall quickly, but none of them would be alive afterward to take advantage of the fact.

"Let's just get this done," Wesley said. He swung his pick and drove the point into the mortar between two bricks. Rollie did the same. Randall knelt on the ground and started working at some of the lower bricks, and now Wesley understood why he had rags tied around his knees, to pad them against the stone floor. The *chink chink* of their picks striking sounded like a series of chimes. *Music of the mines*, he thought.

8

Cordelia paced the lobby, trying to keep her blood flowing in order to stay awake. *It's almost funny,* she thought. *I'm trying so hard to wake Wes up, and all I want to do is curl up and go to sleep for about a year. What if he's just a really sound sleeper?*

Even as she thought it, though, she knew it wasn't true. Her mind had been playing tricks on her for the last hour or so, spiraling off onto random tangents, scanning information without really reading it. She had been trying to read a passage she'd found about sleeping spells, and realized finally that she had read four pages without retaining a single word she'd seen there. So she tried to wake herself up. She crossed to the hotel door and stepped outside, breathing in the cool night air. She turned on a radio and found the hardest rock station she could find, cranking up the volume. Every now and then the deejay came on and took calls from listeners, and

Cordelia knew that she wasn't the only person awake in the city after all, that there were many others—some up by choice, because of their jobs or just their own internal schedules, some unable to sleep because of worry or chemistry or some other reason.

But that knowledge didn't help her stay awake. She brewed yet another cup of strong tea and paced some more as it cooled, slapping her cheeks lightly as she traced her path across the floor. Once she even pinched the flesh of her forearm, but that just hurt and didn't do much to help her alertness, so she gave up on that tactic.

Finally, the computer chimed again, and she hurried to it, opening the E-mail even as she sank down onto her chair. This was the one she'd been waiting for. Franklin Ayers Bishop had come through.

"Cordelia," he had written. "Following is a recipe, if you will, for an immunity potion you or your partners can make. This won't wake Wesley, but it will prevent the Calynthia mix from affecting anyone who takes it. I will continue working on some means of waking those already under its spell.

"In the meantime, I have contacted a network of friends—wizards and witches and sorcerers around the world—and asked them to bring their own powers to bear on the situation in Los Angeles as well. There are strong emanations from that part of the world tonight, and I fear that powerful magicks are at work there. Rest assured, the problem is being investigated and I will continue to report to you as progress is made."

Below that she found his "recipe," an assortment of commonly-found substances that could be combined, in a ritualistic fashion, to make the immunity potion he had promised.

She hit the PRINT button and waited, all thoughts of going to sleep banished from her mind.

Five O'Clock

1

Cordy dialed Angel's cell phone number and paced as his phone rang, the paper on which she'd printed Bishop's instructions quivering ever so slightly in her hand as she walked up and down next to Wesley's sleeping form. Finally, she heard Angel's voice on the other end.

"Angel—" she began.

"Is something wrong?" he interrupted.

"No, nothing like that. No change in Wesley's condition. I'm calling with good news, I think."

"What is it?" he asked.

"An immunity formula," Cordelia told him. "Wesley's friend in New Zealand came through, and there's a way you can immunize yourself against the effects of Calynthia powder."

"Even if we don't know how it's been altered?" Angel asked, sounding suspicious of her news.

"That's what he says. You'd have to know what's been done to it to counter the spell, to wake Wesley or anyone else up once they've been dosed with it. But not to prevent it from working on you. You just need to drink some of this goop he describes."

"Okay," Angel said. "How do we make it? Is it complicated?"

"Slow down, boss," Cordelia said. "And listen up. You're going to have to pick up some ingredients."

"At a magick shop?"

"I don't think so. Are you writing this down?"

"I'll remember," he promised.

Cordelia wasn't sure she trusted him to do that, but didn't want to belabor the point. The morning was coming, and Angel functioned better in the dark than under the sun. She took a deep breath, knowing how well this was going to go over. "You need chocolate milk," she said. "And lemon-lime soda, raw eggs, Tabasco sauce, and a dash of motor oil."

There was a long moment of silence from Angel's end.

"Are you sure this is an immunity potion?" he asked, at length. "Sounds like it's designed to purge, rather than prevent."

"I know how it sounds," she said. "He says there's some ingredient in each of these things that's necessary for the potion. You could just use the specific ingredients and make something that's a little more palatable, but it'd take ten times as long to find everything and put it all together. He's offering a substitute formula using commonly-found substances so you can do it in a hurry."

"Remind me to thank him later," Angel said, "if I survive it. What about the measurements?"

"Apparently very flexible," Cordelia replied. "A little of this, some of that. Kind of like those old recipes calling for pinches and dashes. I guess whatever sounds good."

"There's no stretch of the imagination in which it sounds good."

"When you have everything mixed together," Cordelia continued, ignoring his protest, "you need to stand with it facing in each of the compass directions. Drip a little on the ground at each compass point. When you drip it to north and south, say these words: 'Slumber not.' When you drip to east and west, say 'Let no potion cause me harm.' Then you drink some."

"Sounds simple enough."

"Bishop said you could say it in Latin if you wanted to—that's the traditional way to go—but he doesn't think it's really necessary. It's one of those symbolic acts . . . just as symbolic if you say it in English, but it sounds fancier in Latin."

STRANGER TO THE SUN

"Is this guy for real, Cordelia?"

"I don't know, Angel. He's a friend of Wesley's. He's offering help when no one else is. Can we afford to ignore him when he might be our best chance?"

"I guess not," Angel said. "It doesn't sound like any magick I've ever heard of, that's all."

"Well, maybe he has a point about the symbolism," Cordelia said. "Wesley is always explaining that magick is all about doing something small in a way that affects the larger world. Same principle as a voodoo doll, I guess. So maybe since magick all stands for something else anyway, it doesn't really matter if you go in for all the excess ritual."

"I don't know," Angel said. "But we don't have a lot of time to test the theory. If it works, great. If it doesn't . . . then we'll have a serious problem."

"Bishop says he's in contact with some other magicians around the world. They're trying to come up with a back-up plan. But if you need to go up against these guys and they've got the Calynthia, you'll need something like this."

"Okay, Cordy. We'll try it."

He hung up, leaving Cordelia with a dead phone in her hands. *Angel is right,* she thought. *Bishop's recipe sounds insane. Even if someone could keep it down, what good could it possibly do?*

And had she done more harm than good by passing it on to Angel? If he assumed it worked and relied on it against a Calynthia attack, and it didn't work . . . then they'd all be a lot worse off than before.

2

Angel mentally checked off the list Cordelia had read him. *Chocolate milk, lemon-lime soda, eggs, Tabasco, motor oil. Delicious. At least he could have worked a little type A into the mix, for flavor.*

He put the phone away and saw Gunn looking at him, a questioning expression on his face. It was the first time since hearing about Cosmo's close call, and the argument with Rio, that there had been any expression other than fury on Gunn's face, so Angel was glad to see it. "Cordelia gave me a formula," he said. "For immunity against the Calynthia."

"Judgin' from your face, it don't look tasty." His tone was flat, not as sarcastic as it would have been under better circumstances.

"It doesn't sound tasty." He told Gunn what they needed to do.

Gunn shook his head sadly. "Nasty," he said. "Truly, truly foul. Cordy wouldn't play a practical joke, time like this, would she?"

"No," Angel said simply, changing lanes. They were heading south on the 110, in the direction of the Rosecrans neighborhood the vampire had described. But traffic had come to an abrupt halt—night work on the freeway had narrowed the lanes down to one, and the resulting congestion had slowed traffic considerably. Three vehicles behind them was the War Wagon, camouflaged to look as much like a regular, civilian truck as possible. Behind that was the white van with the rest of the crew in it.

"No, I know she wouldn't. Just wishin' she was. We have to drink that stuff?"

"Would it be better if we had to slather it on our bodies?"

Gunn thought that over for a moment. "I'll drink," he decided. "There's an all-night convenience store not far from here. Seems like they'd have most of that stuff. I don't suppose Eggbeaters would do in a pinch?"

"She did specify raw eggs," Angel clarified. "I think we should stick with the real things."

"Well, they might have some," Gunn said. "I can tell you now, my boys aren't gonna like it."

"Do they like anything?" Angel asked. "They seem kind of negative to me, overall. And aren't some of your boys actually girls?"

"Yeah, and yeah. They tend to be negative, 'specially when there's a vampire around they can't kill. You been through what they have, you'd be negative too. They almost lost one of their own, tonight.

They've lost others in the past." He seemed to think about that a moment. "Well, you have been through it, pretty much. And a lot of people would interpret dark and broody as negative, know what I'm sayin'?"

"I suppose," Angel admitted. He inched forward. They were close enough to the construction site now to see the big equipment, trucks and cement mixers and bright lights on tall stanchions. The concrete had been poured already and the workers were in the process of smoothing it out. It wasn't long before L.A.'s real rush hour would start, and the work crew would want to have at least one more lane open by then, and maybe two. The fast lane, on the far left, would have to stay closed for at least a day or two in order for the concrete to dry, and the result would be increased congestion on L.A.'s already strained-to-the-limits roadways. *Another reason the sewer tunnels are sometimes an improvement,* Angel thought. *Hardly any traffic jams down there.*

"And yeah, some of 'em are female," Gunn added, somewhat defensively. "I just use 'boys' like 'the guys,' you know. The gang, the crew."

"I know," Angel told him. "I'm just giving you a hard time. Traffic's got me on edge. Well, that and the fact that we're not any closer to helping Wesley."

"Sure we are," Gunn said. "We're going to make ourselves an oh-so-tasty magick drink and then we'll go kick some vampire booty and save the day."

Angel tapped his hands impatiently on the wheel and took his foot off the brake, moving forward another couple of car lengths. "You make it sound so easy."

3

Gunn had been right about the convenience store. Once they'd made it through the freeway logjam, it had been just off the second exit. Its lights stood like proud beacons against the night, as if the shop offered world peace and an end to poverty instead of just gas, milk, bread, beverages, and junk food. When Angel went in, a clerk was busily pouring coffee into massive filters and shoving the filter baskets into big coffee pots. Four fresh pots already sat on warmers, one decaf and three regular, filling the store with their aroma.

"Morning," the clerk said wearily. He wore a red, white, and blue short-sleeved polyester uniform smock over a long-sleeved T-shirt, and looked about nineteen. His five o'clock shadow—five in the morning, but five nonetheless—and tired eyes testified to the fact that he was nearing the end of a shift, not beginning one. "Coffee's fresh."

"No thanks," Angel said. But some of Gunn's crew came in behind him and headed for the coffee pots and the displays of fresh muffins and doughnuts and Danishes. Angel couldn't deny feeling some hunger pangs himself, surrounded by all this food, but he was pretty sure blood wasn't in the store's inventory. Instead, he did his best to ignore the exclamations of the guys loading up on snacks and went to gather the items Cordelia had said they'd need for the immunization.

In spite of all the business Angel had brought in, the clerk made him pay for a large, empty soda cup in which to mix the formula, in addition to the ingredients he purchased. But he got outside first, and while the rest were finishing up their own transactions, he sat in the parking lot pouring together the bizarre concoction. Since Cordelia had not specified amounts, he went heavier on chocolate milk than he did on Tabasco sauce or motor oil. None of it mixed well, and he ended up with a nearly black semi-fluid with mysterious chunks floating in it.

When he was finished he did as Cordelia had instructed, turning to each point of the compass and spilling a little on the ground. *Where it belongs,* he thought. He spoke the prescribed phrases, "Slumber not," and "Let no potion cause me harm," as he poured. When there were four splashes of the rank mixture on the asphalt, he raised the cup to his lips and took a drink.

"*Eeeyuchh,*" he said, making a face. "That is really bad."

Gunn had come outside and watched him. Angel handed him the cup. "Drink up," he said.

"I got to?"

"Unless you want to fall asleep the first time they spray Calynthia at you," Angel reminded him. "And if you fall asleep in their lair, who knows what they'll do to you."

"I'm drinking," Gunn said resignedly. "I'm drinking, okay?" He performed the ritual, tilted the cup, and took a big swallow, then held it away from himself. "Oh, man. Know what you said?"

"I think it was something like '*Eeeyuchh.*'"

"Yeah. Same goes for me. I think it'd be easier to get used to a hemoglobin diet than this stuff."

"Everybody has to drink some," Angel reminded him, "or they'll be vulnerable to the Calynthia."

"They ain't gonna like it, but I guess they'd like the big sleep even less."

As the crew filed out of the store with purchases in hand, Gunn called them over and passed the cup, explaining how the ritual had to be performed. Each of them in turn made the proper motions, spoke the appropriate words, and tried to keep the foul mixture down.

Rondell went last, and when he was finished the cup was empty. He carried it to an outside trash container, wiping his mouth with the back of his hand. "Man," he said. "That does it. I gotta drink that swill, I'm damn well gonna kill me something tonight."

"There's not much night left," Gunn pointed out. "Let's roll."

4

Rio watched the ritual from the darkness outside the glow cast by the convenience store's bright lights. He couldn't be sure what they were up to, just that they were all drinking something from the same cup, which couldn't be all that sanitary. And whatever it was, it wasn't particularly delicious either, judging from the expressions on their faces. The vamp had been the one who mixed it, and Rio didn't trust him for a second. He wondered if there was a way that vamps could turn other people into bloodsuckers without biting them, just by feeding them some kind of magickal elixir. He'd never heard of anything like that, but until a couple of months before he'd thought vampires just existed in old black-and-white movies and books admired by Goth chicks.

Gunn insisted that this vamp was different and they could count on him to be straight up. And there had been a time when Rio had trusted Gunn. That had ended tonight, though, when Gunn sided with Angel against him and banished him from the crew for the simple act of killing a vampire—which was

STRANGER TO THE SUN

supposed to be what they were all about. The vamp
had already told Angel and Gunn everything she
knew; Rio had heard her desperate confession even
in the hallway, so anxious was she to betray her
friend and save her own inhuman skin. Bringing her
along wouldn't have accomplished anything except
giving her a chance to escape and feed on more
humans.

Given that, he was glad he'd been forced out of
the crew. He wanted to work with people who wanted to kill vampires, not coddle them. When he'd had
to stake Janice he had accepted a new calling in
life—he would be a vampire hunter until the day
that he died. When Gunn and the guys had helped
him out against his first real nest, he thought he'd
found kindred spirits. But maybe not—Gunn was
always going on about how it was more complicated
than just finding them and dusting them, even
though it looked just that straightforward to Rio.

Still, he knew that there was killing to be done
tonight, and lots of it, most likely. So when he left
the hotel, he walked around the block, out of sight
of the War Wagon or anyone else in the crew, and
jacked a parked car. Even in Alamogordo, people
knew how to hotwire a ride, and Rio had done it a
time or two before. He had carefully pulled the car
up to a corner of Rosecrans, a couple of blocks away
from the hotel and turned the car's lights out. He
waited until everyone had piled into the War

Wagon, the van, and Angel's old boat, and then he'd followed them at a safe distance. Having heard the vampire's statement, he knew approximately where they were going, but he hadn't been in town all that long and figured they stood a better chance of finding the right warehouse in Downey than he did alone. He'd let them do the hard part, and then he'd go in and kill himself some bloodsuckers.

So the night wouldn't be a total waste after all.

5

Working cautiously, never taking full swings or hitting the bricks too hard for fear of sparks, Wesley and Rollie tore away at the mortar holding the old coal-blackened bricks in place. After a time of this, there was a space big enough for a lantern to be passed through. Wesley held his hand out for one—his own was still out and would remain so, since striking a match to re-light it could easily set off the firedamp.

"Pass me a lantern," he said quietly.

The boy, Randall, handed his over. Wesley lifted it cautiously—its flame grew and blued as it neared the ceiling—and held it out through the hole they'd made in the brick wall. It didn't cast much light, but the shaft looked passable as far as he could tell.

"It seems clear," he announced. "No sign of cave-in,

at any rate." He handed Randall back his lantern. "Let's get the rest of these bricks out of the way."

Hands free, he began pulling at the bricks. At this point it was safer to break them off the wall by hand than to continue striking them with a pick and risk a spark. Rollie put down his own pick and joined in. But Davies just growled.

"We leave 'ere and go wanderin' about in old shafts, they'll never find us," he argued. "Ye know they're already diggin' for us, right?"

"We do know that," Rollie countered. "But we also know that we have no idea how much damage was done in the cave-in, or if they'll be able t'reach us in time. If I'm t'die it'll be tryin' t'live, not layin' down and givin' up."

"So ye'd rather die lost in the pits than 'ere, where at least your body could be found. Me, I'd rather 'ave a decent burial. I've a woman, ye know, on the outside. I think she'd like to see me one last time. What about the rest o' ye?"

"My ma would want to see my body," Randall said. "My pa died in the mines, two years gone now. She said his body brought her comfort 'cause at least she knowed he weren't lost forever."

"For my part," Dafydd put in, "me family's far from 'ere and accustomed to the minin' life. They don't 'ear from me, they'll know what 'appened."

"None of us has to die," Wesley insisted, rocking another brick and breaking the mortar that glued it down. The top three feet of the wall had been cleared away now, and he could taste stale air from the other side. "If this shaft has been bricked in, there may be enough good air in it to dilute the methane. We can live long enough to find a way out, and we'll all see our loved ones again."

"Wesley, pull here," Rollie said. "You lot, stand back. I think if we put our weight into it, man, we can take down th'rest of it all at once."

Wesley put his hands where Rollie indicated. He thought the miner was right—the bricks were more solidly set against one another than they were against the sides and floor of the tunnel. They leaned against the wall with all their weight and then gripped the back sides of the bricks, pulling toward themselves, trying to rock the entire wall free instead of concentrating on a single brick at a time. It gave under their efforts, scraping against the tunnel walls on either side. An inch, then another, then several all at once. *It's going*, he thought with a sudden flash of happiness. *It's really going.*

"Stand clear, boys!" Rollie called out. He and Wesley gave a mighty tug, and the wall came toward them, bricks buckling as the wall pulled away from the tunnel sides that had helped firm it up. With a crash, the wall fell inward. Bricks slammed into Wesley's ribs, stomach, and legs. They'd leave bruises, but he barely felt the impacts, knowing that they had made a positive step toward freedom and survival.

At least, he hoped they had. If Davies was right, though, they were about to embark on a journey that would only end with them lost inside mine shafts none of them knew their way around, trapped down here in the never-ending dark until the lack of air or water or food did them in. Unless an explosion or cave-in brought them merciful relief from slow death.

He knew he couldn't afford to think that way, though. He needed to keep trying and not let negativism win the day. *A positive effort is always better than simply giving in,* he thought.

"Come on, then," he said, trying to sound cheerful. "Let's not waste any more time here."

"Go on," Davies said. His arms were crossed and his mouth set in a thin, determined line. "I'll stay 'ere and tell 'em where to look for your bodies."

He's more stubborn than Cordy is, Wesley thought. It didn't seem particularly strange to him that he knew Cordy was stubborn but couldn't remember exactly who Cordy was, or even if the name belonged to a man or a woman. *Maybe it's someone I knew once in a dream,* he thought. "We've got to stick together," Wesley argued. "We may all need each other before we're out of here."

"If we go up that shaft we'll never *get* out."

"Look," Wesley snapped. He was becoming exasperated with this man, verging on letting him stay behind after all. "If you don't believe we're making progress after a short while, we can come back here. What do we have to lose by taking a look?"

Davies shuffled his feet a little and glanced up the shaft, and Wesley knew the recalcitrant fellow was ready to give in. "What if we can't find our way back?" he asked.

"If we're forced to make any choices, we'll mark the walls," Wesley offered. "We'll score them with our picks so we know from which direction we came."

"That good enough, Davies?" Rollie asked.

"It is for me," Randall said.

"And me as well," Dafydd agreed.

"Right, then," Davies said. He didn't sound convinced but he was at least tired of arguing. "Let's go if we're goin'."

With Wesley in the lead, they made their way up the shaft, which angled slightly toward the surface. Soon enough, they found that beyond the range of their lanterns, the shaft made a sharp turn to the left and then, less than a dozen meters later, dead-ended at an intersection with another, slightly wider tunnel.

"Which way here?" Wesley asked. This tunnel seemed to be level, not rising or falling. He'd been hoping to keep climbing toward the surface, but obviously that wasn't going to be an option.

Rollie, once again, stepped up to the rescue. "I say left," he said. "From where we were before, the main pit was t'the left. So if this one intersects with that on some other level, it'd be that way."

"Very well," Wesley said, using the point of his pick to mark the left corner, about shoulder high. Since the walls were black no matter how far one dug in, he carved a quick X shape which anyone would be able to feel with a hand. "This one's marked. We go left."

"I just 'ope we can find that again."

"I hope we won't have to," Randall added.

"I'm with you on that one," Wesley said. "Let's hope we never see this shaft again."

He led off to the left, still holding Randall's lantern, which the young man had generously allowed him to keep while he carried Wesley's defunct one. This shaft, like the last, had obviously been well-worked—seams of coal dug out to the solid stone beneath. The stone floor still showed the nicks and scars of clogs and the buckets that the coal was put in when it was pulled from the walls. *Some relief, at least,* he thought. Just knowing that people had walked this tunnel at some point in the past gave him cause to believe there might be a way out in addition to the bricked-up passage they'd come through. And the air tasted better, he realized—fresher than it had been before. As a test, he raised the lantern to shoulder height. The flame remained steady and yellow.

"Look," he said. "Methane's dissipated."

For the first time since the cave-in, Wesley's optimism became more real than forced. *We might just get out of this yet,* he thought.

Which was when the tunnel dead-ended at a massive, recent rockfall.

6

"Must be the place," Gunn said in a low voice. They'd been driving the blocks on and around Rosecrans, in Downey—but Rosecrans was one of those Los Angeles thoroughfares that goes on for miles and miles, and limiting it to Downey helped only if one was convinced that the vampire who'd tipped them to it actually had her city limits designations down. Finally, they saw a few young people in outlandish outfits straggling to their cars, looking worn out after a long night. The kids seemed to be coming from what looked like an abandoned warehouse, graffiti-covered and with trash strewn around its perimeter. "Matches what that vamp told us."

"We'll take a closer look," Angel suggested. "She said the vampires were meeting behind the club, in an underground room or something." He drove around the seemingly empty building. But it was not empty—as they got closer they could feel, then hear, the *thump-thump* of a driving bass beat. The music inside must have been nearly deafening. Angel noticed Gunn's head bobbing slightly in time to the beat. "Yeah, I guess this is the place," he agreed. He pulled the GTX into the dark loading area of a warehouse down the block. The War Wagon and the van followed, and Gunn's crew spilled from both, weapons in hand. From the backseat Angel took a broadsword, while Gunn retrieved his hubcap-axe. The still-weak Cosmo would stay behind in the van, accompanied by a tough, burly little guy named Kool, so their number was down by three from earlier, including Rio.

Angel looked around at the somber-faced vampire hunters. "I don't really know what we're up against in there," he said. "But I know it's important to find out."

"If it's about killing vamps, we're down with it," Chain said.

"Thing about these boys havin' a one-track mind," Gunn observed, "you can count on 'em to be consistent."

"There's something to be said for that," Angel said.

When everyone was armed, Angel led the way across the street. Driving around the building had shown only two ways in—the front door, which seemed to be the entrance to the rave, and the loading dock in back. Angel had decided the loading dock was the best bet. He tried to pierce the darkness with his gaze. Whatever lurked inside there was somehow involved with Wesley's mysterious slumber, he was certain. *Time to find out what's going on in this town.*

Two doors seemed to lead inside from the dock—a massive rolling steel door and a smaller pedestrian door. The big door seemed like too much effort and noise, so they went in through the small door, single file. When they were all inside, the last person in the line pushed it closed, and they stood in the dark trying to let their eyes acclimate. Angel knew that Los Angeles threw as much light skyward at night as the full moon cast upon the Earth, so during their nocturnal excursions they had never been in absolute darkness.

Until now.

There was no light at all in the room. Angel couldn't tell how big it was—even his extraordinarily keen night vision wasn't sufficient to cut through this blackness. They had decided against turning on their flashlights, figuring that, at least at first, flashlights would serve more to make them targets than anything else. Gunn's crew made a bit of noise, scuffling and breathing, but not enough to be heard over the music blasting from the club next door. *We may be blind but at least we still have surprise on our side,* Angel thought.

Which was when he heard the faintest sound—a kind of spinning, whistling sound, coming toward him, barely audible beneath the music. The sound of a projectile of some kind. He whipped his sword up in a defensive posture and something struck its blade, shattering on impact, like glass. Angel felt himself sprayed with a fine mist when it hit. *Got to be the Calynthia. Guess it's time to find out if Cordy's potion really works,* he thought.

So far, so good. He remained on his feet and alert. "We're under attack!" he shouted. More Calynthia bombs hit the floor around them, some even slamming into the crew. There were shouts of pain in the dark, but no one fell asleep under the assault. "Lights!" Angel called. They were already targets, and they needed to see where their foes were. Several of the guys clicked on flashlights and pointed them around the room, finally settling on a dozen vampires nestled in the overhead rafters, hurling down the Calynthia bombs. Judging by their expressions, they were figuring out that the Calynthia was not having the desired effect.

"Let 'em have it!" someone called. Crossbows were raised and wooden bolts darted toward the overhead framework. A few found their marks, and vamps exploded into dust. The surviving vampires snarled and dropped from the heights, landing on their feet. Fangs bared, they rushed the band of vampire hunters.

Angel braced himself, spreading his legs wide for balance and swinging the big sword as the vampires charged. His steel sliced through a vamp neck and the attacker's head spun off, head and body blowing into simultaneously smaller and larger clouds of dust. Beside him he saw Gunn swing upward with his axe, splitting a vampire in two and then finishing with a coup de grace that beheaded him. *Another dusted,* Angel thought. When two more went down, he started to believe this would be easier than he'd dared hope.

Two of Gunn's guys met the oncoming vamps with stakes in their fists, eliminating two more vamps from the planet forever. One vamp swung a powerful arm, clawing George and knocking him backward a dozen feet. In the darkness, Angel couldn't see if George was hurt, but he stepped up and beheaded the vampire before it could pass through their line and get behind them.

Three more targeted him as he separated himself from the others, though, hitting him high and low at the same time. He felt their fingers dig into his chest and biceps as they drew him, like a snared fish, toward the out-thrust fangs of the third, his sword clattering uselessly to the cement floor. Angel planted his feet for stability and drove his skull forward into the vamp's teeth. The vampire gave a screech as teeth and jawbone shattered.

Angel yanked away from that one and gripped the other two. One hand on each, he slammed them into each other. Hands darted at him again but he dodged this time, shaking his arms to release the spring-loaded stakes up his sleeves. He lunged forward and dusted the two vamps grasping at him. The third one, still shaken from Angel's headbutt, staggered blindly, and Angel finished him off almost casually.

Then he looked around to see that the rest of the crew had vanquished their opponents with a minimum of damage. George had suffered a cut on his forehead that bled down into his right eye, but Albert was helping him tie a bandanna over it to soak up the bleeding. Albert had a series of deep gouges down his left arm. Angel had been cut, but his wounds were already beginning to heal.

Breathing hard from effort, Gunn came over and put his hand on Angel's shoulder. "That wasn't so bad," he said. "Is that what all this was about?"

"Can't be," Angel said, shaking his head. "That was just a warm-up, the first line of defense. We still haven't seen the real enemy."

"You're mixin' your metaphors, man," Gunn said with a chuckle. "This a game or a war?"

Angel stifled a grin. *I had fun,* he thought. But he couldn't say that to Gunn; he didn't want to downplay the risk involved. "If anyone thinks it's a game they should leave now," he said somberly. He pointed a flashlight at a staircase that led down from this level. "Because that's where we're going. And when we go down there, it'll be deadly serious." *Emphasis on "deadly."*

Their vampire informant had told them that the action tonight was taking place *under* the warehouse, not *inside* the warehouse. Since her information had proven accurate so far, Angel had no reason to think it wouldn't continue to. Now that the upstairs guards were wiped out, they needed to get downstairs. And fast, since there was every indication that the key to reviving Wesley lay down there.

"Let's go," he said. Their battlefield ministrations finished, the others lined up behind Angel and they headed for the stairs. There was a kind of pit in the center of the room, with a short flight of concrete stairs leading down into it. Angel descended first, and found a door inside the pit. Behind the door, a stairway led down a dozen steps and then did a sharp one-eighty. He couldn't see what happened there, but guessed that it went down some more, into the unknown. Angel played a flashlight briefly over the stairs before starting down, to make sure they weren't booby-trapped in any way. He saw electrical light fixtures mounted along the ceiling, but switching on the lights was the surest way to alert anyone below that they were coming. Except for the lights, the stairway was unadorned poured concrete, without even a handrail. He turned the flashlight off and stepped into the dark, moving surely yet silently down stairs he couldn't see.

When he reached the landing he could vaguely

hear, in dramatic counterpoint to the driving beat from the rave just behind the walls, what sounded like an ancient religious service of some kind. There was a single droning voice chanting words in a language Angel couldn't make out, interrupted every now and then by many voices chanting some kind of response. *At least it'll be hard for them to hear us coming,* he thought. *If they were counting on those guards to stop anyone before they reached the stairs, we should have surprise on our side.*

Considering the number of voices he heard, surprise would be their only advantage. It sure wouldn't be numbers.

When the stairs came to an end after two more landings, the chanting was louder but the darkness still complete. Angel shielded the flashlight with his hand and flicked it on for a fraction of a second, just enough to get the lay of the land and to indicate to those still descending where he was, so they didn't all stumble over him.

They had ended up in a kind of plain concrete alcove. Two large steel doors lay between them and the chanting voices. No light leaked through the doors, just the muffled sounds of chanting, and something else, two mingled odors that were so familiar but faint that it took Angel a moment to place them.

The scent of vampires, a unique smell. And the powerful, bewitching scent of fresh human blood.

Convinced that the doors were light-proof, Angel turned on his light again, so everyone could see him. He gestured toward the doors.

"They're through here," he whispered. "I think there are a lot of them, but there's no way to know how many until we get in there. It's going to be a hard fight."

"We're ready," Rondell said with quiet determination. "We got plenty to pay them back for."

"Okay, then," Angel replied. "Let's do this."

7

Rio watched them disappear into the dark warehouse, single file, weapons raised against whatever might lie in wait inside. He couldn't help wishing he was with them. He was a team player—football was his sport, not track or tennis or any of those games that pitted one individual against another. He liked the way that everybody brought their own skills to the table—in his case, upper body strength, quick legs, and the determination to keep going against any odds and never give up. He loved the camaraderie of a team, enjoyed the good-natured, playful give-and-take, swapping insults and towel slaps in the locker room but coming together and functioning as a single, cohesive unit on the field. He figured military service must be a lot like that, and he'd given thought to enlisting.

Until the Janice incident had changed the course of his life forever. That had taught him that there was an enemy more insidious, more purely evil than anything an army could ever face. If the government even knew vampires existed—*and they must,* he thought. *How could they know so much about what went on within their borders without knowing about this?*—he suspected they'd keep the knowledge closely guarded. Maybe, at best, a few specialized units would be sent after the bloodsuckers, but the main branches of the military could never know because they'd never be able to keep the secret. The whole world would soon know, and panic would ensue.

Or would it, he wondered. Maybe the populace would take it in stride if they knew that a major offensive was being launched to curtail the activity. But then again, he figured most people had a deep, instinctive revulsion to vampires, and they might not calmly accept proof of their existence. It was a complicated issue, and he was not, he decided, a complicated guy. Better brains than his were required to figure out the best way to proceed.

Fortunately, those weren't decisions he needed to make. He just needed to get inside that warehouse and help with the killing that was sure to happen. He gave Gunn and his crew fifteen minutes to get

things started, and then he dashed across the street
and through the door he'd seen the others use.

8

At Angel's word, they burst through the doors. He
charged in first, sword held high, screaming an
ancient Irish war cry he hadn't even known he
remembered until it rose within his throat as if trig-
gered by battle-lust. The others took it up, or voiced
their own contemporary versions of it. They sounded like a ferocious horde rather than a dozen brave
but frightened young men and one old but youthful
vampire.

The place they entered was a large chamber,
high-ceilinged, with dozens of pillars to support the
weight of the concrete floor above them. It was lit
by what seemed to be hundreds, maybe thousands,
of candles, their scents mingling with those of the
blood and the bloodsuckers. And it was full of vampires.

They lined the walls, stood among the candles,
and filed past the tables in the center of the room
where two humans had obviously been sacrificed for
whatever ritual was taking place here.

In what was clearly a position of importance, the
object of attention of most of the vamps until the

screaming force charged in, a tall, handsome vampire stood by himself, hands raised in the air, a strange luminous globe hovering in the air before him. He barely cast a glance at the doorway and then launched into his chant once again. Angel thought he detected a new note of urgency in the vampire's voice.

Then he was beyond any such critical thinking and lost in battle. The vamps met their charge with a countercharge of their own. Mostly without weapons, they met the onrushing warriors with fangs, pitting pure vampiric strength against human-honed wood and steel.

The air was full of shouting voices, full-throated screams of rage and fear and pain. Angel's blade whirled and flashed as he drew a deadly figure-eight pattern in the air. Every place it intersected a vampire, a head flew and another vamp burst into dust. Through the chaos, he could see Gunn, determination heightened by the injuries to several of his friends, plowing through the vampiric horde with his axe. No vamp could stand up to his steady onslaught. Rondell and Albert carried long-handled wooden stakes, short spears, almost, and, side by side, battled their way into the chamber. Someone else used a crossbow, loading wooden bolts into it with mechanical precision and taking fast but careful aim to ensure that each one sailed true. Still another fighter spun a wooden pole with both ends sharpened to points, a vicious combination of quarterstaff and stake.

But in spite of the seemingly overwhelming advance, the vampires had the advantage of vastly superior numbers. For every one dusted, another three or more could take its place. Instead of backing down, they came on, hissing and clawing. Angel realized he was gradually becoming spattered with blood—some of his own but more splashed upon him by his human allies, wounded in the fight. He suffered his own wounds—a punch here, a fang there, a stake that he spotted just in time to turn away from so that it embedded in his shoulder instead of his chest. Each time he was injured he dusted his attacker, but he knew that the sheer number of wounds was slowing him down, making him lose focus and control at some level. Assuming the same was happening to his human allies, they would certainly be hindered even more.

Angel continued to slash away with his sword. There were so many vampires it almost seemed that he didn't have to aim; just hacking blindly he cleared a path through them that Gunn and his crew could follow. All the while, he tried to keep an eye on the tall vampire at the back of the room. The globe continued to glow and spin before him, and he kept up the steady chanting, as if he couldn't risk being interrupted at this point in whatever ritual he performed.

Which makes it that much more important to interrupt him, Angel thought. The vamp was clearly the centerpiece of tonight's entertainment, and the globe probably a representation of what it was he was magickally accomplishing. Angel still didn't have enough information to connect this with what had happened to Wesley, but he was sure that a connection existed, and that was enough for him. He made the tall vampire his target, and began to direct his efforts to clearing the way toward him.

As Angel watched him, the vampire glanced away from the spinning globe and locked eyes with him for a moment. Angel could read two things in those eyes—the vampire was supremely confident of his ritual's potency, and just as worried that it would be cut short before it was finished. Everything about the vamp—his size, his bearing, his obvious physical strength—indicated that he'd be a formidable foe when they met in battle. *And we will meet,* Angel swore to himself. *I'll make sure of that.*

With this new goal firmly set in his mind, he redoubled his efforts, slashing his way through the vampires that swarmed around him like a bear through bees, determined to get the honey they guarded.

Six O'Clock

1

Cordelia sat next to Wesley, holding the slumbering man's hand in both of hers. Exhaustion had set in; she envied the easy way he slept while everyone around him worked to find out how to wake him. *Maybe he doesn't want to wake up,* she thought. *Maybe he's just a really disciplined sleeper, and he'll wake up in the morning feeling really refreshed, wondering what all the fuss was about.*

But she knew it didn't work that way; that was just tired-brain thinking. She had seen him go down, suddenly, under the spell of the magickal Calynthia potion. There had been nothing natural about it. Still, he slept on and she couldn't help wishing she could join him. She figured if she climbed into the bed with him and he woke up, she'd have some awkward explaining to do. And if Angel and Gunn came back while she was still in there, she'd never live it down. So she stayed in the chair, trying to remain upright, but she let her eyes close, just to rest them a little. A minute later her head drooped toward her chest.

The chime of her computer startled her awake. She brought her head up suddenly, blinking to dispel the grogginess, and gently rested Wesley's hand back on his chest. She had never thought she'd turn into one of those geeks more excited by an E-mail than, say, a phone call from a casting director or a handsome and wealthy man, or even a handsome and wealthy casting director. But right now she wanted good news more than anything else, including a date or an acting job. And good news seemed most likely to come in the form of an E-mail, so she hurried to the computer and read what had come in from Franklin Ayers Bishop.

"Cordelia," he wrote. "With the help of colleagues at different locations around the world, I am afraid I've figured out what someone in your vicinity is up to, and it's not good news."

So much for that brief notion, she thought.

"To be quite succinct, somebody there is trying to shift the axis of the earth. I'm not entirely sure to what end yet, but the result would likely be catastrophic—earthquakes, tidal waves, global climate change, with one pole melting and raising sea level dramatically, while the other one expands its reach and creates a new, localized ice age. Suffice to say, it can't be allowed to happen.

"I am working with my contacts to see that it does not. The magick is strong, though, and countering it from such a distance is difficult. I will try to keep you informed of our progress, but now must return to the task at hand."

Cordelia held her breath as she read, and then blew it out in frustration when she got to the end and realized that all she had received was even more bad news. *Isn't anything going to go right tonight?* She called Angel's cell phone to update him but got no answer.

She went back to Wesley's side and sank into the chair, feeling more defeated now than she had before. Her drowsiness was gone, but the fatigue she felt to her bones was worse than ever.

2

MacKenna could only rush the ritual so much. The required words had to be said—to skip even one syllable of the unfamiliar phrasing, memorized by rote since this language was never meant to be spoken by the tongues of humans or once-humans, might be to invite disaster. But as soon as the doors burst open and the attackers came into the pool of candlelight, he recognized Angel. The vampire with a soul, they said, the vampire who hunts his own kind as mercilessly as he once did humans, when he went by the name of Angelus. The one who had missed being ensnared in his web, this night. *That explains why Homer and Lenny never came back*, he thought. *Either they haven't found him yet—or they did. In which case they'll never be back.*

So he sped up as much as he could, careful to pronounce each syllable but running the words together, maintaining the chanting tone he had practiced. The chanted responses were carried by fewer voices now as the other participants rushed to meet the attack, but he didn't think that mattered. The energy was contained within him; his was the voice that really counted. And as he continued the ritual, the globe before him continued to tilt—turning one side away from the sun's toxic glow, forever.

MacKenna thought at first that his legion of followers—far outnumbering the intruders—would easily best Angel and his band. But he stole glimpses of the battle when he dared, and so far it didn't look like that was the case after all. With every glance, it appeared that Angel was closer and closer.

He tried to put the vampire's advance out of his mind, fearful that it might distract him in these crucial last moments of the ritual. Speaking as quickly as he dared, he hurried through to the ritual's final utterances. The globe-image before him tilted still more, and then winked from existence.

And so it was done. A vampire homeland was made, a land of eternal darkness. Vampires would never again have to fear the sun. But the humans trapped in the vampire's territory of night—they would have plenty to fear.

Enough self-congratulation, MacKenna thought. He looked toward the battle, and couldn't see Angel. *Has he finally gone down?* he wondered, hoping against hope. But no—a moment later Angel surfaced, throwing off three vampires who had tried to pin him. His sword flashed like liquid silver, and the vampires exploded into dust. Angel's gaze rested on MacKenna.

Time to go, he thought. *Victory can't be savored if I don't survive the moment.*

If he had to make his way through the fighting, he knew, he'd never get out unscathed. But there was another exit, an escape route no one but his most trusted acolytes knew of, hidden in the back wall behind a stack of empty boxes placed for comouflage. Turning his back on Angel and his friends, MacKenna ran for that wall. He threw the boxes aside and opened the door. A dark staircase beckoned.

3

"Angel!" Gunn shouted. When he had the vampire's attention, he pointed toward the back wall, where the guy who seemed to be the head vamp was making a break for it. But before he could see Angel's response, if any, he had to swing his axe up in a sideways arc that took off the upper portion of an oncoming vamp's right shoulder and head. That vamp exploded into dust, and two more charged through the dust cloud.

Gunn couldn't remember ever having been in such a furious battle in his long career killing vampires. Usually the attacks were short and sweet. Vampire nests—when the bloodsuckers could stand being near one another at all—tended to contain less than a dozen vamps. Even if the vampires fought hard, they were pretty evenly matched by the guys in Gunn's crew and the toughest of them would go down after five or ten minutes of pitched fighting. But here, there were probably a hundred of the creatures. He and his guys were vastly outnumbered. On the positive side, when his gang killed them all—if they managed to kill them all instead of being killed themselves—they'd have made a pretty good dent in the vampire population of Los Angeles.

The strange thing was that the vamps, generally a fairly cowardly lot, were fighting to the death, as if trying to protect something really important to them. Which made it that much more crucial to beat them down and find out what it was they were guarding.

Gunn could tell that Angel had already decided the key was the head guy, the one who was escaping even now, and the glowing green orb that had floated in front of him until just a couple of minutes ago. Angel worked his way toward that area with single-minded ferocity, and Gunn tried to cover Angel's flank as best he could. But now he was locked in combat with a handful of his own opponents, and Angel was, for the moment, on his own.

There were three of them on Gunn now, in too close for the axe to do him any good. Their hot breath in his face stank like spoiled meat and their hands tore at him. *This is where the invulnerability of a superhero would come in handy*, he thought. He let go of the axe's handle and the weapon clattered to the floor as he drew a stake from his belt. But strong hands grasped his arms, fingernails digging into his flesh, and he couldn't bring it up high enough to do any damage. As he struggled, their grips tightened and one of the vamps leaned in, its sharp fangs brushing his neck.

"You're a powerful one," he heard the vamp whisper just below his ear. "You'll make a fine snack."

Gunn tried to twist and writhe his way out of their clutches, but he couldn't—the combination of his own weariness and their supernatural strength was too much for him to overcome. He tried to brace himself for the end that was coming, tried to tell himself that by dying this way, going down fighting, he wasn't betraying the memory of Alonna, the sister he'd had to stake when she had been made a vampire. He felt the fangs pierce his flesh—

—and then the vamp they belonged to burst into dust. In surprise, the two holding him let their grips weaken for a moment, and Gunn took advantage of that moment to lift the stake and drive it through the heart of the one on his right. Turning to dust the other one, he saw who his rescuer was—Rio, grinning like Ed McMahon himself had just knocked on his door with one of those giant-sized checks in his hands.

"Thanks, dog," Gunn said breathlessly.

"No prob, dude," Rio said. "Just wanted to kill me some bloodsuckers, you know?"

"Kill away," Gunn said, glad for the extra pair of hands. Glad that he still had his own life. Maybe he'd misjudged Rio, after all.

But he didn't have a lot of time to dwell on it. The vamps kept on coming. He jabbed another with the stake, and then another, though it seemed like an endless tide of them. Glancing over, he saw that Angel was in a position pretty much like he had been—completely swarmed, almost buried in vamps.

But Rio was charging to Angel's side, his sharp stake dusting one vamp after another. He'd have to reconsider his decision to fire Rio from the team— guy seemed like a definite asset after all. As Gunn watched, Rio and Angel worked together, polishing off the vampires one by one until they stood, for a moment, together in a circle of empty space, all the vamps near them either occupied by fighting others or making a run for it.

Angel nodded at Rio, and Rio took a quick step toward him, putting out his right hand as if offering to shake Angel's. Gunn saw the uncertainty in Angel's eyes, and he started to say something him- self, but then a vamp slammed into him and it was all he could do to fight that one off.

4

Angel didn't know where Rio had come from—or why, for that matter, he'd returned after being eject- ed from Gunn's group. At the moment he didn't care a whole lot about those issues, because Rio had just helped him fight off a concentrated attack by several vampires who had come perilously close to burying a stake in his own heart. Now, in the moment's respite they'd bought, Rio stretched a hand out toward him like he wanted to shake, maybe to make up. Seemed like bad timing to Angel—the room was still full of live vamps. But maybe it was important to the kid. After a moment's hesitation, he moved his sword to his left hand and put out his own right, meaning to make it a quick slapping of palms and then back to business.

But Rio grabbed his hand and squeezed, moving in even closer at the same time. His left hand went around Angel's back, and the thought that Rio still held a stake in that hand crossed Angel's mind. Looking into Rio's eyes, he suddenly saw the young man's malicious intent revealed there. Even as he felt Rio's stake graze against his back and Rio lean into him for leverage, Angel brought his left elbow up in a short, brutal arc that slammed into Rio's nose and mouth.

Rio staggered back a couple of steps and Angel followed that blow with a right to Rio's chin. The kid's head snapped back and his legs folded. He sank to the cement floor. Angel thrust with his sword, realizing only at the last possible moment what he was doing and stopping the motion. Rio had tried to kill him, but the guy was a human, not a vampire or demon. Drawing the sword away, Angel instead lashed out with the heel of one of his boots, cracking Rio across the bridge of the nose as he tried to regain his feet. This time, he went down to stay, unconscious but not dead.

Now he took a moment to look at what Gunn had

pointed to a minute earlier—the doorway that had swallowed up the tall vampire who had been performing the ritual when they came in. Just beyond the doorway he could see an almost hidden staircase, some escape route the vampire had no doubt had ready in case of attack. Other vamps, seeing the possibility of a safe retreat, followed.

Angel knew the tall vamp was the key to everything and couldn't be allowed to get away now. He released a stake into his left hand and used it to dust vamps while he slashed with the sword in his right. Gunn seemed to understand the urgency, and he sped up his efforts as well, both of them working their way through the seemingly endless supply of vampires faster than ever. They left Rio behind on the floor. Angel hoped the guy was safe from the vamps back there, but wasn't about to waste too much energy worrying about him.

A moment later, Angel decided that the supply of vampires did indeed have an end, if only because so many of them were retreating up the far stairway rather than continuing the fight. All around them, Gunn's crew polished off the few remaining vampires, and then they stood alone in the suddenly-deserted room. Everyone had suffered some wounds, but the worst was Albert, whose right arm had been broken, the bone jutting out through bloody and ragged flesh. Angel spared him the briefest of glances and then started for the far door, behind the last of the retreating vampires. Behind him, he heard Gunn's voice.

"Yo, Albert, get back to the van and get Kool to take a look at that. And get Rio outta here. Rest o' you, follow Angel!"

5

At the top of the stairs there was another door. On the stairwell side the door had a handle, but on the other, MacKenna knew, it looked like a blank panel of wall-board, scribbled on and stickered, no doubt, by the kids who frequented the rave club and considered such things the pinnacle of artistic achievement.

Because this emergency exit opened directly onto the club's dance floor.

When he threw the door open and charged through, he emerged into another world. The vast warehouse space was almost dark except for black lights and bright white lights that occasionally strobed across the floor. Between the strobing flashes, various items glowed under the black lights—patterns on clothing, stickers on walls, glow sticks and plastic jewelry. MacKenna even saw a girl dancing with her mouth open and her pierced tongue glowing a sickly yellow-green color, painted with some substance he hoped was toxic.

More striking than the darkness—for MacKenna had come to love the dark—was the music. So loud it almost had solid form, a veritable wall of sound, it brutalized his more-sensitive-than-human hearing and disoriented him. He shoved his way through the throngs of dancers, still going strong at this hour of the morning. He couldn't imagine mere humans having the powers of endurance that would keep them on their feet and moving this long, but figured it must have something to do with the sheer volume of the music preventing them from collapse. The humans he passed stank of stale sweat, and he barely felt tempted by the blood that coursed in their veins as he shoved them aside on his way toward the door.

6

As soon as he passed through the upstairs door Angel realized the genius of the vampire's escape route. By entering the club and mingling with the teens, still moving to the music's insistent rhythm, the vamps had rendered Gunn's crew essentially useless. In this poor light, they couldn't necessarily tell vampire from raver, and they wouldn't stake people at random hoping to find the right ones. Angel himself could see well enough in the dark club, but he couldn't spare the time to point out every vamp to the human vampire hunters.

Halfway across the club floor, and getting farther away all the time, Angel was able to make out the tall vampire heading for the club's outside door. The vampire pushed his way through the dancers, but the path he made closed up behind him. With no other option, Angel began the same process. As he shoved through, young people gave him dirty looks, and a bold few pushed back, but for the most part the dancers were passive, even gentle. He heard a few whispered comments, but they were more on the order of complaints about his rudeness, not words directed at him in anger. For all their black clothes, leather, piercings, tattoos, and nonconformist hairstyles, Angel realized that these rave kids were a pretty nonthreatening bunch.

Which meant that the tall vampire made quick progress as he plowed his way through them, even more ruthless in his advance than Angel was. As he went, Angel noticed that his own progress was duplicated by some of the vamps, also moving toward the door and an escape to the outside. He couldn't worry about them, though. The tall one needed to be captured, the full extent of his plan discovered. The image of Wesley asleep in the Hyperion's lobby hovered near the forefront of Angel's thoughts, and the tall one was the key. He was sure of that.

"What do we do, man?" George asked.

Gunn shrugged. "I can't see jack," he said. "I guess we go slow and stake who we can. But we better be doggone sure who's a vamp and who ain't before we dust anybody."

"It looks like they all changed back to human," Rondell reported, emerging from the crowd. "All I see out there are people, you know? Not a fang or bumpy forehead in sight."

"Okay," Gunn said, sounding resigned. "Change of plans, then. We'll have to get our tails outside. When they come out we can get a better look at 'em. After the sun comes up, the rave kids'll go home. These clubs always close near dawn, way I hear it. Vamps will be afraid to go outside then, and if there's anybody left inside we can just come back in and finish 'em off."

"Some of these kids look pretty pale," George said. "And check out that makeup. Sure we can't stake a few of them, just for good measure?"

"We go around stabbin' kids with wooden sticks, we're gonna have a lot to answer to," Gunn countered. "More than we want to deal with. Come on. Let's get outside and see what comes out." Without another word, he stepped into the writhing throng and began weaving his way toward the exit.

8

Angel finally broke through the last knot of kids blocking the doorway and dashed outside, past a muscular, sleepy-eyed bouncer who barely registered his presence. He couldn't see anyone on the dark streets, but he heard footfalls, maybe a block away. Someone in a big hurry.

Angel was in a hurry too. He ran at top speed, ducking down the nearest side street to follow the sound. The night had been long and frustrating and he could use a pint of O pos for energy, but the knowledge that the enemy who might hold the key to saving Wesley was getting away spurred him on.

In a few moments he came out onto another major street that ran parallel to Rosecrans. The warehouse district hadn't really come to life yet, though it would soon, and traffic was still limited to a few random cars and trucks. But there, two blocks away and receding into the distance, was the tall vampire he had seen downstairs.

Angel had never bothered to clock himself. He knew that, since becoming a vampire, his strength and speed were far beyond what he had enjoyed as a human. And he continued to train, to make sure his muscles were strong and limber, his senses sharp, his reflexes keen. He couldn't outrun a cheetah at top speed, he knew. Probably not even a thoroughbred racehorse. But there were no humans he couldn't best, and very few other beings, vampires or otherwise.

This morning, though, he ran as he never had before. Head down, arms and legs pumping in perfect rhythm, he landed on the balls of his feet and pushed off with all his strength. *Better shoes might help,* he thought at one point. *Boots aren't the best way to go for speed.* He was reminded of Gunn's costume suggestion, and wondered briefly if track shoes were part of the traditional superhero outfit. Despite the footwear drawback, he made good time, swallowing ground quickly. He only raised his head to make sure his course was clear and that the vamp was still ahead of him.

A couple of times, he caught the tall vampire glancing back over his shoulder, fear beginning to show on his face as Angel closed the gap between them, little by little.

The tall one had long legs and an easy stride, but he didn't seem to have Angel's stamina. The more he slowed, the more worried he became and the more often he looked back to see Angel gaining, always gaining. The tall vamp's legs began to fail him, knees bumping each other, his feet not landing squarely, and that slowed him even more.

Finally, nine blocks from the club, Angel pulled within reach. The tall vamp seemed to know it, because he suddenly stopped and swiveled and filled his fist with a sharp wooden stake. Momentum carried Angel into him, and the stake drove deep into his chest. When he didn't explode into dust, Angel let out a short laugh.

"You missed."

The vamp tugged his stake out and shoved Angel away with the same powerful motion. Angel fell back onto the sidewalk, weakened by the wound even though it had cleared his heart. Tucking the stake back into his belt, the other vamp picked up a metal trash can that had been left out on the sidewalk by a merchant and hurled it at Angel. Angel swatted the thing away, sending garbage flying into the street, and struggled to his feet.

"I've heard about you," the vampire said. "The exalted Angel. The vampire with a soul. The vampire who hates himself so much he attacks those like him and tries to fit in with the meat."

"That's not exactly the way I look at it," Angel said, glad the vamp felt like running off at the mouth, because it gave him a chance to recover slightly from his wound. His most recent wound—there had been many of them, over the course of the night.

"Of course not," the vamp went on. "Because you delude yourself. You delude and you deny. There's nothing unusual about that, except perhaps the extent of your delusion."

"You seem to know a lot about me," Angel goaded.

"Just by reputation, until now. And you are a

fierce fighter, I'll give you that. You made a good try, down there, you and your little meatbag friends. But your efforts went for naught. Too little, too late, isn't that the phrase?"

"Something like that," Angel replied. His strength was ebbing back, moment by moment. "Why? Too late for what? And, since you have the advantage of knowing my name, who are you?"

"I am called MacKenna."

Angel nodded. "Ah, yes. Heard of you too. Hear you think you're pretty special."

"Not *think*, Angel. *Am*. Look up at the sky, turn-coat."

Angel glanced up. It was the sky. Nothing earth-shattering that he could see. "What about it?"

"It should be brightening by now, don't you see? The sun should be rising in the east, there should be a glow just over there, a band of light across the horizon. It's not there. Nor will it ever be."

Angel couldn't resist taking another look. MacKenna was right. It was after six. The sky was just as dark as it had been all night. "Is this what you've been up to?" he asked. "You've been messing with the sun? You have no idea what kind of forces you're—"

"But I do know, Angel. I know precisely what I've done. And I know what the results will be. Massive loss of life. Human life, that is. And a permanent dark zone, the new homeland of the undead. You're in the capital of the dark zone, right here. Who do you suppose the vampire community will look to as their natural leader? The one who gave them this paradise on Earth."

"The stories were right," Angel said. "You *are* insane."

"Wrong. Completely sane and rational. You think I have delusions of grandeur, Angel. But in fact, I am not deluded. I truly am the bringer of a new world in which vampires will reign supreme."

"It'll never work," Angel insisted.

"It already has. The sky is proof enough."

"What did putting people to sleep have to do with it?" Angel asked him.

MacKenna seemed happy to go on talking, as long as Angel prompted him. Angel was still in pain, but quickly regaining strength. Still, he feigned weakness, leaning against a wall as MacKenna went on. Even as he gathered his resources, though, he felt a sick feeling in the pit of his stomach. If MacKenna was right—and the dark sky seemed to bear him out—then he had irreversibly altered the Earth's proper alignment, and the devastation would be unthinkable. "Two things," MacKenna said. "I was able to channel their life force, the energy they would have used had they been awake, and to a more limited extent the power they put into what must have been remarkably realistic dreams. This supplemental power enabled me to complete the ritual when no one else has ever been able to do so."

"And you chose as targets those people—astronomers, occultists, and so on—who would have been most likely to realize what was happening in time to stop you," Angel finished.

"Another great old cliché comes to mind: Two birds with one stone. It's a beautiful thing."

"Pretty smart," Angel admitted. "And what happens to them now?"

MacKenna shrugged. "They'll wake up, if their constitutions are strong enough. Maybe some won't. No great loss. Most of targets were humans. If they wake up, it will be to a world where they're nothing more than food." He laughed, a truly sinister sound. "Humans on the hoof."

"Sounds like you have it all worked out," Angel told him.

"It's not too late for you to embrace your nature," MacKenna said. "You think I'm telling you all this because I like to gloat? To hear my own voice? I'm a practical man, Angel. I haven't survived this long by being verbose. I could use an associate with your particular talents. You could sit at my right hand. Enforcer, aide, chief of staff . . . make up your own title."

"You know," Angel said calmly, "I'm not proud to be a vampire. I'm not proud of a lot of the things I've done since becoming one. But there are moments that I'm glad I am, because if I weren't"—

He coiled his muscles, keeping his eyes locked on MacKenna, trying to look casual while holding the vamp's gaze with his own—"I wouldn't be able to do this!"

Angel jumped across the sidewalk, closing the gap that separated them faster than MacKenna could react. They both went down in the street. Angel struggled to get his hands around MacKenna's throat. The other vamp jabbed at Angel's face with a thumb, trying to gouge out an eye. Angel vamped out, letting his forehead swell and provide more protection for his eyes. But as he scrambled for a hold, MacKenna got a knee under him and slammed it into Angel's chest, knocking him aside.

Both vampires gained their feet and faced each other at the edge of the street. MacKenna had drawn his stake again, and held it out before him like a dagger. Big trucks, eighteen-wheelers, were parked along the side of the road, and the two vamps occupied an empty space where one of them must have pulled out earlier. A single truck-length that Angel was determined would be MacKenna's final resting place.

He circled MacKenna, and the other vamp turned warily, alert for any move Angel might make.

"This is a mistake, Angel," he said quietly. "I'm no enemy of yours."

"That's where you're wrong, MacKenna."

Another big truck rumbled past as they spoke.

MacKenna's eyes ticked toward it for a moment, and Angel made a move toward him. But MacKenna recovered and responded to Angel's move, jabbing with the stake. Angel backed away again. *This could take all night,* he thought. A moment's glance at the sky confirmed that it still *was* night, with no signs yet of morning. The possibility came to him that all this was pointless—the damage already done, taking out MacKenna could only provide him an instant's gratification. MacKenna was right—a place where the sun never rose would become a haven for vampires, and some form of leadership would rise up to provide structure. If it wasn't MacKenna, it would be someone else just as bad.

But sometimes, he thought, *an instant's gratification has to be good enough.*

He charged again. MacKenna met his attack with the stake but Angel turned sideways to it, letting it sink into his left arm in order to neutralize its threat. At the same time, he brought his right fist around in a powerful hook, putting his shoulder and most of his weight into it. The fist drove into MacKenna's jaw with the force of a pile driver. The tall vamp rocked backward, his skull bouncing off the grille of the truck parked behind him. Angel brought his hand around again, backhanding MacKenna as he tried to shake off the first shot. MacKenna staggered out into the street.

Right in the path of an oncoming big rig.

The driver hit his air brakes but had no room to

stop, and tons of steel slammed into MacKenna at forty miles per hour. The truck shuddered along for another fifty feet before coming to a full stop, and MacKenna was dragged part of the way, then thrown onto a parked car. He bounced off the car and up against the stone wall of a building. Finally, he sank to the sidewalk.

Angel pulled the stake from his arm and ran to MacKenna's side, waving off the trucker, who was beginning to climb down from his cab. "Don't worry about him," Angel said. "He'll be fine."

"But . . . but I hit him," the driver replied, his voice quaking with emotion.

"Yeah, he'll be all right." Angel helped MacKenna to his feet. He was battered and bruised, cut in a dozen places, but after a couple of staggered steps he blinked and looked at the trucker himself, raising a hand as if to show he was okay.

The trucker hurried back into his cab and slammed the door, then hit the gas, racing away even faster than he had arrived.

"That . . . hurt . . . ," MacKenna said through his broken mouth.

"Not as much as this," Angel replied. He brought up MacKenna's own stake and drove it through the vampire's heart. MacKenna's face took on a startled aspect, as if he couldn't quite believe Angel still wanted to kill him, and then he exploded into dust.

Angel wiped the gritty remains of the vampire off

him and stared at the sky. Still no sign of dawn. The sun was no friend to him, but he still hoped he'd see it again.

9

Wesley's initial hunch had proved to be a mistake. They had taken the tunnel they'd found in the direction that would have intersected with the main shaft currently in use, but that way had been closed by rockfall at some point. So they had turned and gone back the other way. Eventually, the other shaft began to angle upward more steeply. After walking along it for quite a while, they seemed to be making good progress but in entirely the wrong direction.

"What do you think?" Wesley asked finally. "Have we made another wrong turn?"

"Could be," Rollie replied. "But I'm not sure. The old shafts didn't always connect t'the main pit. If they're old enough, they might predate the main pit, which was only dug nine years ago, give or take."

"So where would they have come out, then?" Wesley asked him.

The older miner just shrugged. "The ground around here is a warren o' tunnels. Wasn't it your neighbor, Davies, what wound up in a tunnel tryin' t'take a bath?"

"Aye," Davies said with a sharp laugh. "Filled the basin wi' 'ot water and climbed in, 'e did. But 'e turned out to be too 'eavy for 'is floorboards, which 'ad been laid over an old mine openin'. The 'ole basin fell through, 'im in it, and 'e landed down in the tunnel. 'E was all right, but I don't think 'e ever took another bath as long as 'e lived. I 'ad to move away from 'im, as I was startin' to smell 'im through the walls."

While it was clear that Rollie had heard the story before, he broke into a fit of laughter, and Dafydd and Randall joined in, practically doubling over. Wesley enjoyed the easy camaraderie of these men. Their needs seemed to be simple enough—a few bob pay for their work, a drink on the way home, maybe a wife and a child or two waiting when they got there. They lived in the dark and they worked themselves hard, putting their lives in danger. But the shared hardships seemed to draw them together, making them as close-knit as any group of people Wesley could remember knowing.

Of course, he thought with some degree of frustration, *if my memory was whole I'd remember what I was doing yesterday, or before the moment I found myself in the mine office picking up my numbered lantern. I'd remember who these people are and if I've known them before today. I'd remember my*

269

own friends, my co-workers, whoever they might be.
No, memory wasn't to be trusted—he didn't know
much about his situation but he knew that.

Gradually, the shaft sloped up and up, turning
back on itself from time to time. But the lanterns
remained yellow and the air breathable, so they
kept going. With the immediate fear of suffocation
gone, hunger and thirst started to become an issue—
since they had finished their pasties, hours ago,
they'd had nothing to eat, and the little bit of tea
left in their tin canteens was all they had in the way
of drink. Their pace slowed as the effort of lifting a
foot and placing it before the other became more
and more difficult. They persevered, though, Wesley and Rollie taking turns spurring them on, cajol-
ing them, even threatening them to keep the small
group moving.

The tunnel brightened so minutely, little by little,
that Wesley didn't even notice for some time. When
he finally did, he stopped in his tracks. "Look," he
said. "The walls—I can see them without the
lantern. I can even make out the ceiling!"

"Aye," Davies agreed. "It's been like that for a
while now. Been wonderin' when ye'd notice."

"And you didn't say anything?"

"Why? Ain't like we're goin' the wrong way anymore. I said anything, ye'd probably just 'ave
stopped and slowed down our gettin' out of 'ere, like
ye're doin' now."

"Oh, right," Wesley said. "Sorry. Let's carry on, then."

Rollie threw him an amused glance as they continued up the grade. *So apparently everybody noticed but me,* Wesley thought. *Well, it's not like I'm the experienced one or anything.*

Rollie walked close to Wesley as they went, and spoke in quiet tones, for his ears alone. "I don't know who you are, lad, but I owe you a debt of gratitude. We all do."

"Nonsense," Wesley replied. "You didn't need me at all."

"It weren't for you, California, we'd all still be down pit waitin' for someone t'rescue us. And we'd most likely be dead by now, same's that canary. Air down there weren't good enough t'breathe for much longer. But the thing about methane is it saps your reason, as well as your strength. We'd have sat down and given up, thinkin' there were nothin' else for it. You showed us there was a chance, kept insistin' there was hope."

"Well," Wesley said, appreciative of the older man's words. "There's always hope, isn't there?"

"I'd like t'think so," Rollie agreed. "Always have tried t'live that way, and t'teach my brood that, as well."

"You have children?" Wesley asked him, surprised that he hadn't known before. He knew Davies did, and Dafydd was a bachelor, and Randall had mentioned having four sisters and two brothers. Somehow Rollie had kept quiet about his own family, though it did seem familiar to Wesley after a moment.

"A girl and a boy," Rollie said. "Imps, both of 'em. But sweet, too, when they calm down. Which is only when they're sleepin', most often."

As he spoke, they followed the tunnel around a sharp bend, and at the end of a short length, sunlight streamed in.

They all hurried to the exit, tired muscles not willing to run but too excited to walk, so that they settled on a kind of jog to the shaft's exit. The sun beamed in at them, its rays warm and welcoming after so long in the dark. Wesley teared up at the brightness and shut his eyes momentarily, then opened them in a squint to let them adjust to the light.

They had come out on a low hill overlooking the town, which lay before them looking almost as black with soot as the mine itself. Immediately below the base of the hill, mine workings were visible, and a throng of people were gathered, women and children as well as miners.

"They're waitin' for us," Rollie said. "Waitin' for some word, be we alive or dead."

"I wonder if there are still others trapped down pit," Randall said.

"I suppose we'll find out," Wesley said. As they

spoke, someone on the ground below caught sight of them and let out a scream. Others looked up, and shouts were raised as the mass of people began to move uphill like a wave washing up the slope of a beach. Wesley saw people dressed in their finest clothes, women in long dresses and men in suits and hats. Photographers with massive box cameras on spindly-legged tripods gathered their gear and joined the swarm, eager to snap the first photos of the survivors.

Rollie turned to Wesley and extended his right hand as if to shake. "Thank you, Wesley, for all you've done."

Wesley reached for him, but instead of feeling solid flesh, his hand passed through Rollie as if through smoke. The entire scene seemed to be fading out, Rollie and Dafydd and Randall and Davies becoming pale, even transparent, and the crowd below, the city, the hills themselves all emptying of color. Fading to white . . .

1 0

Cordelia had stepped away from Wesley for a few minutes to brew a fresh pot of coffee. Angel and Gunn would likely be returning soon, since it was well past six and the sun would be rising. They'd be tired but wouldn't be ready to sleep unless they had made some positive progress on the Wesley situation. *And,* she thought sadly, *that doesn't seem all that likely.*

The last half hour or so had been bad. Wes had shown no signs of waking, but he'd begun to sweat in his sleep, and thrashed about like he was fighting something. "Or dancing," she said aloud. "I've seen you dance. You're no Angel, but you're no Baryshnikov either."

Then the thrashing had stopped, and he had lain almost preternaturally still, his right eye twitching occasionally, but showing no other signs of life other than the continued, steady rise and fall of his chest as he breathed. This was almost worse, she decided, because it more closely resembled death.

As the coffee began to drip into the pot, filling the air with its rich scent, her computer chimed once again. She turned away from Wesley and java and went to the screen. After the last E-mail from Bishop, she was almost afraid to read this one. But the heading was "SUCCESS!", and her heart skipped a beat when she saw it. She clicked to open it, then sat down to read.

"Dear Cordelia," Bishop wrote. "I have good news, for a change. The ring of magicians I told you of has successfully counteracted the spell originating from there in Los Angeles. As I mentioned previously, it was difficult, because the magician working there was powerful and we were all a great distance away. But—and I am only guessing here—because he was trying to influence the whole of the Earth and we were spread out at many points across the planet, we were able to hold the Earth in its proper place and even to restore what little progress he had made before we became aware.

"I am not entirely certain, but I believe we had some help in this effort from a source unknown to us. Had the magician there completely and properly performed the ritual, all might have been lost. I do not think he missed much of it—he was certainly making some headway before we stopped him—but perhaps he was interrupted at some point, or mistakenly bypassed some part of the spell, because there was a point at which we suddenly were able to gain a foothold. After that, nothing he did would have made the difference.

"At any rate, if you look out a window, you should start to see the sun rising in the east, as it is supposed to do. Thank you for alerting us to the problem, and for providing support throughout the process, as well as for taking care of Wesley. I do hope that he recovers soon—I shall keep working on the Calynthia problem, but do let me know if there is any improvement.

"Kind regards, Franklin Ayers Bishop."

"Wes!" Cordy shouted when she reached the end. "He's done it! They've done it!" She dashed to the door and threw it open, looking out toward the eastern horizon. Sure enough, dawn's light broke the solid black layer of sky. She came back in. "They really did do it!"

"That's wonderful," Wesley said, his voice thick and groggy. He pushed himself up onto his elbows. "Who has done what?" He blinked a couple of times, as if orienting himself. "And what the devil am I doing in a bed in the lobby?"

"Wes!" Cordy shrieked, louder this time. *He's awake!* She ran to him and threw her arms around him. "You're okay!" She squeezed him tight, until he began tapping her shoulder and she saw that his face was turning kind of blue.

"Sorry," she said, releasing him. He took a gasping breath. "*Are* you okay?"

"I believe so, yes." His voice was clearer, and he seemed alert and aware. *Both good things,* Cordelia thought. He pushed the blankets off and sat up on the edge of the bed. "Were you worried that I might not be?"

"Well, yeah," she replied. "You did this whole Rip van Winkle number on us."

"Rip van . . . ," Wesley began.

"You know, American folktale. All about sleeping and, well, I'm not all that clear on the details myself, but I didn't want to say Sleeping Beauty. If you make me, though . . ."

"I was asleep?" Wesley asked, sounding surprised

at the news. "I guess that explains the bed. For how long?"

"Ten hours, more or less," she told him. "Do you remember anything? Opening the package for Angel? Do you remember me telling you not to open the package, because it was for Angel?"

"I remember you telling me not to open the package, but it was because you wanted to do the honors, I believe. Not because it was addressed to Angel."

"Okay," she said, resigned. "So your memory's intact. Big whoop."

"Wait a minute," Wesley went on. He stood up, still a bit unsteady on his feet. But he seemed able to move around well enough. "I've been asleep for ten hours? Here, in the hotel lobby?"

"Dead to the world," Cordelia confirmed. "Although I didn't really want to use that word. 'Dead,' I mean, but now that I think about it, 'world' was a touchy concept for a while there, too. You owe Franklin Bishop a big thank you, I can tell you that."

"You're going to have to slow down a bit, Cordelia," he said. "Because I've had the strangest experience, and because I can't quite grasp whatever it is you're babbling about."

"Okay," she agreed. "I'll spoon-feed it to you, all right? You, sleepyhead. Me, research gal. Angel and Gunn—well, other than driving around all night and having to drink some truly heinous mixture, I'm not sure what they're doing. Speaking of which, I should call them. And I should E-mail Bishop. And—"

"What happened to the part about slowing down?" Wesley asked.

"Just keep up, okay?" Cordelia used her exasperated voice, just to let him know how glad she was that things were back to normal. "You're a smart guy, you can do it if you try. Especially since, out of all of us, you're the only one who's had a good night's sleep."

Epilogue

The front door burst open and Angel stormed in, followed by a glum-faced Gunn. "Better pack your bags, Cordelia," Angel said. "We blew it."

"What do you mean, blew it?" she asked brightly. "And aren't you going to say, 'Hi, Wes'?"

"Hi, Wes," Angel said. "You pack too."

It was Cordelia's turn to be confused. "Wait, slow down," she urged. "Communicate in full sentences. What do you mean, you blew it? And you might try to show a little pleasure at the fact that Wesley's alive and well."

"I didn't get to MacKenna in time," Angel said. "He tilted the Earth. Our side doesn't face the sun anymore, and as soon as the vampires figure it out, you're all in trouble."

Cordelia studied his dour face for a minute, long enough to determine that he wasn't joking. *Or if he is, he's really pulling it off,* she thought. Then another thought occurred to her. "Angel, do you have the top up on the car?"

"Yeah," he said after a moment's thought. "Why?"

"Take a look outside," she said. "A careful one, though."

Gunn turned and beat him to the door. "What do you know?" he said, sounding considerably more cheerful than he had looked when he'd come in. "Sun."

"Sun?" Angel echoed wearily.

"What it looks like to me."

"There's sun?" Angel asked again.

"Look for yourself if you don't believe me," Gunn said. "But like the lady said, carefully. Seein' as how you have a tendency to burst into flames, and all."

Angel peered through the door, long enough to see the brightness in the sky. "But . . . but I didn't stop MacKenna."

"You didn't have to," Cordelia informed him. "Apparently you slowed him down or made him lose his place or something. But whatever you did, it was enough to let this friend of Wesley's—"

"Franklin Ayers Bishop," Wesley put in, sounding like he was finally coming to understand.

"That's right," Cordy continued. "Him. He and a bunch of other wizards or warlocks or whatever were working from all over the world to hold the Earth in place. He says that whatever you did gave them the chance they needed to get a grip on it, or something. And they reversed the damage the bad guy had done, so everything's okay. And then Wesley woke up, so everything's super okay."

Gunn put out a fist and Wesley tapped it with his own fist. "Good to see you up and around, English," Gunn said.

"Apparently it's good to be up and around," Wesley said. "Although, frankly, it sounds as if I slept through all the trouble and didn't have a thing to worry about."

"Nice work if you can get it," Gunn said with a smile.

"Wesley," Angel said a bit more seriously, "I'm glad you're back. We missed you." He paced around the lobby for a moment, looking at the front door, the bed where Wesley had slept, the computer. "I still don't get it, though. I didn't get him in time. I saw the globe tilt. The sky stayed dark."

"It doesn't matter," Cordelia insisted. "They fixed things, that's what counts. Oh, and Wesley's awake, that counts too."

"Thank you, Cordelia," Wesley said. "And thank you for, presumably, raiding my E-mail address book and telling complete strangers about our problems."

"Worked out, didn't it?" Cordelia asked.

"It seems to have," he agreed reluctantly.

"So what were y'all doin' while we were out fightin' bloodsuckers and tryin' to save the world,

Wes? Sleepin' like a baby? Have any bad dreams, at least?"

Wesley smiled, a wry grin that Cordelia knew well. The grin that indicated there was a lot more behind it than he was letting on. "Funny you should ask," he said.

By the time Wesley was done with his story, he had sat down on one of the blue banquettes in the lobby. Gunn leaned against the front counter, Angel sat backwards on the chair Cordelia had put next to Wesley's bed, and Cordy herself sat cross-legged on the bed listening in what was, for her, rapt attention, confining her interruptions to only every fifth sentence or so.

"So you led these miners to the sun," she said. "Pretty trippy dream."

"Indeed," Wesley agreed. "However, I can't shake the feeling that it might, in fact, be something more than just a dream."

"What do you mean?" Angel asked. "You were sound asleep, with Cordy watching your every move. What else could it have been?"

"It's just . . . it's hard to explain," Wesley said hesitantly. "Especially since it sounds . . . well, insane, I guess. Certainly unusual, at any rate."

"Well, we're used to that from you," Gunn observed. "So go ahead. Try us."

"Very well." Wesley crossed his arms over his

chest, then realized it might look like a defensive gesture, as if he were afraid he wouldn't be believed. Which was true, but that was not the impression he wanted to project. "I couldn't remember anything about my life while I was there. I knew I didn't really belong there, and every now and then I had a brief flash, when the memories of you all came back to me. That happened less and less as the time went on, and by the time we were really lost in the dark, I couldn't remember you at all.

"The other thing that kept coming and going, but wouldn't stick in my dream-mind, was where I had heard the name Rollie before."

"Where had you?" Cordelia asked. "Short for Roly-Poly?"

"Short for Roland," Wesley corrected. "My maternal great-grandfather's name."

"That must be why it showed up in your dream," Angel suggested.

"I thought that at first," Wesley said. "But the more I thought about it—I mean, the more I try to remember what it was that was nagging at me in the dream—the more I think, maybe not."

"Meaning what?" Cordelia interrupted again.

"Meaning, I haven't thought about my mother's grandfather for quite some time. Years, perhaps decades. I never actually met the man, he had died long before I was born. He was the last on that side of the family to work in the mines—my grandmother said he wanted a different life for his children, particularly after his harrowing adventure with the cave-in. The family spent hours and hours wondering if he was alive or dead."

"So I guess they were glad to see you guys."

"Well, that's the thing," Wesley explained. "They didn't see me."

"What do you mean? You came out with the others, right?"

Wesley didn't address her questions directly. "When I was a boy, my grandparents had some photos on their mantel of my mother's side of the family. My father and his lot never went in much for that sort of thing, but it was important to my mother's parents. At any rate, one of the photos was of four coal miners emerging from a dark mine and blinking in bright sunlight, almost as if they'd never seen anything so bright before. One of them, the miner in the middle, in fact, was my great-grandfather Rollie. I used to look at it for long stretches, wondering what his life had been like. On a few occasions, when my grandfather saw me sitting with it, he told me the story behind it."

"Which you're going to tell us, right?" Gunn asked. "Since you've been talkin' around it for so long now."

Wesley ignored him and went on with his monologue. "The photo had been taken as the men emerged from a mine cave-in, my grandfather told

me. All the miners who had made it out stayed nearby until their fellow miners were accounted for. All
the families of the miners came. The press was
there, the owners of the mine, the mayor . . . it was
quite the to-do, my grandfather said. The photos,
including the one I was looking at, had been taken
by photographers for the newspapers—in those
days, photographers took the pictures but they were
converted into engravings for printing in the papers.
And this one photographer gave his original photograph to my great-grandmother as a souvenir of the
day her husband came out of the Earth."

"This is all fascinating, Wes," Cordelia interrupted, "but do you think you're going to get to the point
sometime today?"

Wesley blew out an exasperated breath. "The
story my granfather told me was that the four men
in the photo said they had been led out of the mine
by someone who then disappeared as soon as they
came out into the sun. Vanished, as if by magick,
they said. None of the family members saw anyone
at all, but all four miners swore by the story. They
said the fellow looked like a miner, like one of them,
but they'd never seen him before that day and they
never saw him again. The story that circulated after
that . . ." Wesley paused, uncomfortable with going
on for the moment. When he spoke again, it was
directly to Angel. "Mind you, I'm not saying this is
the case, by any means—just repeating what my

grandfather told me. They said—well . . ." He stopped again, feeling his own cheeks flush crimson. "This is embarrassing, really," he continued. "They said that the person who guided them from the mine was . . . well, they said he was an angel."

About the Author

Jeff Mariotte is the author of three previous Angel novels, *Close to the Ground*, *Hollywood Noir*, and *Haunted*, as well as, with Nancy Holder, the Buffy/Angel crossover trilogy *Unseen*, and with Maryelizabeth Hart added to the mix, the nonfiction *Angel: The Casefiles: Volume 1*. He's published several other books, and more comic books than he has time to count, including the popular horror/Western series *Desperadoes*. With his wife, the aforementioned Maryelizabeth Hart, and partner Terry Gilman, he co-owns Mysterious Galaxy, a bookstore specializing in science fiction, fantasy, mystery, and horror. He lives in San Diego, California with his family and pets, in a home filled with books, music, toys, and other examples of American pop culture. More about him can be gleaned from www.jeffmariotte.com.

Everyone's got his demons....

ANGEL™

If it takes an eternity, he will make amends.

Original stories based
on the TV show
Created by Joss Whedon
& David Greenwalt

Available from Pocket Books
Published by Simon & Schuster

2311-01

ANGEL™

INVESTIGATIONS:

WE HELP THE HELPLESS

"Los Angeles. It's a city like no other. . . . People are
drawn here. People, and other things. They come for all
kinds of reasons. My reason? It started with a girl."
—Angel, *City Of*

For a hundred years, Angelus offered a brutal death to
everyone he met. And he did it with a song in his heart. A
gypsy curse put a stop to his rampage, but his doomed love
of Buffy the Vampire Slayer drove him from Sunnydale on
his own quest for redemption.

Now, go behind the scenes with your favorite broody vamp
for all of the exclusive dirt. Exclusive interviews with cast
and crew, an introduction by Co-Executive Producer Tim
Minear, episode "dossiers," character files, notable quotes,
color photo inserts, and more!

Everyone's got their demons.

THE CASEFILES, VOLUME ONE
by Nancy Holder, Jeff Mariotte, and Maryelizabeth Hart
Available in June 2002

From Pocket Books
Published by Simon and Schuster